MORE TALES FROM DUST RIVER GULCH

TIM DAVIS

JOURNEY FORTH™

Greenville, South Carolina

Library of Congress Cataloging-in-Publication Data

Davis, Tim, 1957-
   More tales from Dust River Gulch / by Tim Davis.
      p. cm.
   ISBN 1-57924-855-1 (alk. paper)
   [1. Sheriffs—Fiction. 2. Robbers and outlaws—Fiction. 3. Frontier
and pioneer life—West (U.S.)—Fiction. 4. Animals—Fiction. 5. West
(U.S.)—Fiction.] I. Title.
PZ7.D3179 Mo 2002
[Fic]—dc21

                                      2002014353

More Tales from Dust River Gulch

Designed by Miin Ng

Cover and illustrations by Tim Davis

©2003 BJU Press
Greenville, SC 29614

ISBN 1-57924-855-1

15 14 13 12 11 10 9 8 7 6 5 4 3 2 1

**Dedicated
to my family**

Books illustrated by Tim Davis
Pocket Change
Grandpa's Gizmos
The Cranky Blue Crab
Once in Blueberry Dell

Books written and illustrated by Tim Davis
Mice of the Herring Bone
Mice of the Nine Lives
Mice of the Seven Seas
Mice of the Westing Wind, Book 1
Mice of the Westing Wind, Book 2
Tales from Dust River Gulch
More Tales from Dust River Gulch

CONTENTS

WELCOME
TO
DUST RIVER GULCH

Population
13~~0~~ *1*

ATTENTION VISITORS:

Enjoy yerself! Stay a spell!

Sponsored by ROSIE'S RESTAURANT
Home of the Tuesday tomater soup special

CHAPTER ONE

The Lawyer's Suit

Now you gotta understand that the town of Dust River Gulch is sorta like a great big family. 'Course like any sizable family, it's full of characters of all sorts—some more tolerable than others. Take Hare-Brain Jack for instance. . . . Er, on second thought, we'll keep him for later.

Anyway, we've learned to get along here in the ol' Gulch town. When there's no other town any which way closer than a two-day trip through the prairie, you gotta get along—awful lonesome otherwise, don't you know? So we stick together 'round here.

So about Hare-Brain then, maybe you remember the spat he had with the Sheriff a while back? Sheriff J.D. Saddlesoap, that is, finest sheriff this side of the Mississippi, and all-around good mustang, to boot. Now I'm not takin' sides or anythin', but ol' Hare-Brain sure lived up to his name in that big hullaballoo over his carrot patch, now didn't he? Just think of that jackrabbit accusin' the Sheriff hisself of trespassin'! 'Course ever'body knows Jack done had a grudge against J.D. from way back—ever since the sheriff took away his barbering license. But that's another story altogether, and I imagine you've heard it before.

Anyway, like I said, we get along like family here in Dust River Gulch. Got to. So nowadays, you can catch a glimpse of Sheriff J.D. an' that ol' jackrabbit chowin' down together at Rosie's Restaurant from time to time, even sharing a laugh or two. Seems like when trouble comes a-visitin', tryin' to split this town to pieces, it all turns around an' brings us back together. That's 'cause we're family. Guess you got the notion by now.

Well, one particular day, who do you think shows up in Dust River Gulch? None other than Hare-Brain Jack's cousin Harry—the high-falutin' lawyer from Philadelphia (that's back east, you know). Harry came visitin' his jackrabbit cousin, an' it was Harry's first time to be west of the Mississippi, maybe his first time west of the Poconos for all I know. An' he came complainin' like a coyote at full moon.

"Stop this carriage!" he shouts at the stagecoach driver, "before every bone in my achin' body shakes loose!"

With that he steps out into the street, front of Rosie's place, grabs his bag an' stomps off in search of Hare-Brain Jack. He nearly run over Bo the lizard's tail.

"Yikes!" squeals Bo. " 'Scuse me, sir." An' then puttin' on the ol' Gulch charm he asks, "Ken I help you, mister?"

"First of all, you can keep out of my way," says the easterner. "I nearly tripped over you!"

"Sorry," said Bo, hangin' his head.

"Then," continued Harry, "You can direct me to the residence of my cousin Jack. I believe he's the barber in this town."

"You mean Hare-Brain Jack? He's no barber," Bo snickered to hisself.

"Hare-Brain Jack indeed!" Harry snorted, rollin' his eyes.

"Why, you must be Harry," replied Bo with a smile. "Heard you was comin' . . . all the way from back east. Phillerdelburgh, ain't it?"

4

"Philadelphia. And yes, I'm his cousin Harry. Now since you seem to be so intelligent, maybe you can tell me where to find him."

Then just as Bo commenced to answer, Hare-Brain Jack comes burstin' out the doors of Rosie's place. "Harry!" he says smilin'.

"Finally," replied Harry. "Thought I'd have to wander around this intolerable town all day looking for you." Then he kicked Bo's tail out of his way and stomped over to greet his cousin.

"Harry, come on into Rosie's and let's get ourselves a bite to eat," offered Jack. An' with that the two jackrabbits made their way into the best (and only) restaurant in town. You know that Rosie. She keeps the place as tidy as her own kitchen an' serves up the best vittles on this end of the Chisholm Trail.

Well it was Tuesday, an' the special for the day was Rosie's tomater soup. So lots of folks was there. Her tomater soup's good as gold—hee, hee. Jest ask Bo about that sometime. Anyways, Jack an' Harry settled themselves down at the last empty table an' waited to order.

"Never have to wait this long for service in Philadelphia," muttered Harry.

"It'll be worth the wait," replied Jack. "There's no soup in Philadelphia like Rosie's tomater soup."

"I'm sure of that," said Harry with a frown. "Nothing here is anything like Philadelphia!"

"Harry," says Jack, "this town'll grow on ya."

"There's too much of this town on me already," sneered Harry, dusting off his suit.

Then Claude showed up to take their order. Hare-Brain Jack asked for two servin's of Rosie's famous tomater soup.

"Is that all you serve around here?" asked Harry.

"Oh no," laughed Claude. "Rosie cooks up all kinds of chow. Come back tomorrow an' we'll have a different special."

"I'll just have the soup," sighed Harry.

"Nothin' better," added Jack.

Perty soon Claude come back from the kitchen holdin' two delicious bowls of soup high over his head. He was squeezin' his way through the crowded dinin' room like a snake in a corn crib. An' he'd just about got to the jackrabbits' table when it happened.

Now it really weren't nobody's fault what happened. You really can't blame Claude, though Harry sure did. If'n it weren't for that billy goat reaching out to shoo that fly on the backa his neck at just the wrong time—just when Claude was squeezin' by. . . . Well, sometimes things just happen like that, don't they though?

An' if that soup woulda splashed down on most anybody else—some local feller, let's say—he mighta had a good chuckle 'bout it, now wouldn't he? Maybe you recollect that time when Rosie slipped an' slopped a whole pitcher of ice water down the back of Cyrus Skunk? Now he coulda made a big stink about it, but instead he just declared that the sight of Rosie sent chills down his spine. The fellers had a good laugh at that.

Anyway, about that soup an' where it landed. It swirled 'round the rim of Harry's fancy hat. Then it dripped down the fronta his face, down his chin an' all over that perty suit of his. Now I don't know much about fashion, but I reckon that suit was made in a tailor's shop, special-made to fit— like they do back east. An' that suit took in that soup like parched ground takes in rain. Oh, it was thirsty! The fronta that suit was red as a fox afire. So was Harry's face, an' it was gettin' redder by the minute till Harry broke loose with

a mouthful of legal terms that woulda sent ol' Judge Parsons hisself scramblin' to his books.

"Why, I'll sue you till *ipso facto ex statuto ad colligendum defuncti!*" Harry spouted out more litigation than you could find in a court of law in the capitol itself. Now most folks didn't nearly understand what he was sayin' anymore than if he was speakin' Chinese with a Mandarin, but they knew it was trouble for sure. An' they knew that when trouble came to Dust River Gulch, somebody better go get J.D.! So Rosie, she did.

'Fore ya know it, J.D.'s there. "What's the trouble here?" he says.

"You the sheriff?" asked the newcomer.

"That's right."

"I'm Harry, Jack's cousin."

Jack just stared, disbelievin' the whole situation.

Harry continued, "Once I get my lawsuit drawn up, I'll be filing a grievance at your office."

"Lawsuit? Maybe we can tend to yer suit of clothes first, Harry."

"I don't think so, Sheriff. I'm suing this establishment for damages to my Parisian suit, and if it can't pay **full price** for a replacement then I'll shut this place down!" Harry banged his fist on the table.

Well that set the whole place to murmerin' an' mutterin'. Shut down Rosie's place? It weren't even thinkable. But then who knew how much a Parisian suit might cost? The folks in Dust River Gulch didn't know much about Paris, ner any other town in England for that matter, 'cept they knew it weren't easy to get there no how.

"I'm sure we ken work out somethin' better than that," J.D. said, hopin' for the best.

"We'll work it out, Sheriff!" yelled Harry, with soup still drippin' down his nose. "You can count on that! I'll be in your office shortly."

An' with that, Harry stomped out the door. He slammed that door so hard that the big mirror behind Rosie's counter shattered to smithereens an' pictures fell offa the walls. An' Rosie, she started to cry.

"Jack," said J.D. real solemn-like, "You got to have a talk with your cousin."

Hare-Brain nodded, "I'll try, but he can be perty feisty. Guess it runs in the blood."

"Well, *you* came around, Jack. Maybe he will too."

"Hope so," said Jack. An' he shuffled on outta Rosie's a-goin' after Harry.

Well, Jack caught up with Harry an' he spent a good long while explainin' how he'd stirred up that trouble against J.D. a while back. How he'd reckoned him a carrot patch trespasser an' a liar, but in the end he saw different. Jack confessed that he wished he'd never stirred up such a ruckus in the first place. He'd been a fool. An' Jack, he really meant it, ever' bit.

You know a story can be a powerful thing in the tellin', but it can't do much without the listenin' part. It's like throwin' your best seed in the fire—it ain't growin' there. An' Harry was still as hot as a horned toad in the desert sand. He didn't care what Jack told him, an' he wouldn't be swerved from his purpose. He was gonna sue Rosie for every penny she had. Poor Jack, he done tried his best, but Harry wouldn't have none of it.

So Harry drew up his legal papers with every *hereas* an' *wherefore* you can imagine, an' the next day he marched 'em down to J.D.'s office.

"Good morning, Sheriff."

"Mornin', Harry," J.D. scratches his chin an' clears his throat. "Ahemm, I was wondering . . . you done had a talk with Jack, yet?"

"Oh, yes, we've had talks a-plenty," said Harry, "but it didn't take that stain outta my Parisian suit, now did it?"

"I reckon it didn't," J.D. admitted as he shuffled through the legal papers that Harry had brought him. He was lookin' for the bottom line an' wonderin'—what was this gonna cost Rosie? It took ten pages before he got to some language that looked familiar.

"Two thousand dollars?" J.D. hollered, "Rosie don't have that kinda money!"

"Those papers in your hand spell it all out, Sheriff! That tailored suit cost me five hundred dollars when I bought it in Paris. Shipping over a replacement will cost me another seven hundred dollars, and I'm adding on another eight hundred dollars for emotional hardship."

"Emotional what?"

"Hardship, Sheriff. That was my favorite suit."

"Now listen, Harry," said J.D. "I don't know much about Philadelphia, or Paris for that matter, but money don't grow on trees in Dust River Gulch . . . an' there ain't many trees 'round here anyways. Rosie works hard at that there restaurant of hers, but she don't have no two thousand dollars to pay for your suit nor your emotions neither!"

"Then she better be ready to hand over the deed to that property," Harry snorted as he turned for the door, "Good day, Sheriff."

Well, it sure weren't a good day in Dust River Gulch. Pert' near the whole town was gathered over at Rosie's place when J.D. came in. When he told 'em the bad news, they were as low as a wagon wheel in a mud rut. They couldn't imagine the town without Rosie's place. Nobody blamed

Claude, ner the shooin' billy goat, ner even the fly. But there weren't no reasonin' with hard-hearted Harry.

Oh, they was low! But don't you know that the best gold's found down deepest in the mine? It seems like somethin' happened that day in Dust River Gulch. Them folks reached down deep an' pulled up more than they knew was there. I reckon it started with ol' Bo the lizard. After he finished his meal, he plopped his gold nugget down on the counter in fronta' Rosie.

Now you might recall how he came by that prize in the first place. Guess he owed it all to Rosie's famous tomater soup, didn't he? An' it sure did cause quite a stir when that nugget got stolen later on. Reckon I've told them stories before.

Anyway, here he is, ploppin' that hunk of gold right down on the counter. "Don't know if I can make change for that, Bo," said Rosie huntin' in her pockets.

"Oh, I don't want no change, Rosie," Bo replied, swallerin' hard-like. "You keep it. That's a tip for you—for all you done for me . . . an' all of us here in the ol' Gulch town."

"Why, Bo," said Rosie, "you don't mean it."

"Yes'm. I do."

With that Rosie planted a kiss on that lizard's forehead an' said sweet as anythin', "Thank you, Bo."

Bo, he sniffed a little with his hanky and settled back down in the dinin' room. Sometimes a little spark like that can start a whole wildfire ragin' across the plains, an' it sure did that day. Most ever'body left Rosie a real sizable tip for their meal, an' they all came back for lunch an' did the same. Supper too!

In fact, Rosie was collectin' so much extra money, she had to bring out a barrel to put it all in. Tumblewheeze McPhearson took it upon hisself to keep a runnin' tally of the money. From time to time he'd call out the grand total.

By the time Claude had finished washin' the suppertime dishes (an' they was considerable), Tumblewheeze calls out, "Eight hunerd and twenty-one dollars an' seventeen cents!"

"Yahoo!" yells Bo.

"We's gettin' there!"

"That's right."

"Keep it comin'!"

"A couple more days like this an' we might have it," added J.D., smilin' at Rosie like only he could.

"Ya'll have been so sweet," said Rosie, sniffin' with gratitude, "I can't hardly thank you enough."

So as you ken imagine, ever'body slept a little better that night. They weren't outta the hole, but they were startin' to see the top edge. I'd like to think one particular fella' didn't sleep so well—an' that'd be Harry I'm talkin' about. You'd think a twinge of conscience mighta come over him. But then again, maybe some Philadelphia law school done trained that outta him.

Anyway, he shows up at Rosie's place next mornin' with poor Hare-Brain Jack. Harry struts in (wearin' his other fine suit), lookin' the place over like he bought it, or some such-like thing.

"Ah, Sheriff Saddlesoap," Harry says, saunterin' over towards J.D., "I'll be leaving town on the afternoon coach, and of course, I'll expect payment before I go, according to my lawsuit, section four, paragraph thirteen. If those terms aren't met, of course, I'll be expecting the deed to this place."

"This afternoon?" J.D. looked surprised.

Jack shrugged helplessly.

"Yes," replied Harry, "I can only take so much of this town."

"You're takin' more than your share already, far as I can tell," answered J.D.

"Now Sheriff, you know better than that, bein' a man of the law." Harry frowned, "I'm just getting my just compensation. Any judge would agree with me on that."

Just then Tumblewheeze calls out, "One thousand!"

An' there commenced a general celebration 'round the restaurant. All manner of folks congratulatin' each other an' slappin' each other's backs. 'Cept for them two jackrabbits tryin' to figure out what was goin' on.

"One thousand what?" asked Harry.

"One thousand dollars," replied Tumblewheeze, "an' thirty-seven cents."

"Yahoo," added Bo.

"The whole town's been raisin' money to pay for your suit," said Rosie quietly.

"You gotta be kidding!" said Harry, an' his face went pale as a cake of lye soap.

"No kiddin'," said Tumblewheeze. "I've been keepin' tabs, an' it's all rightcheer in this barrel." He jingled a few coins from the collection.

Harry shook his head, disbelievin'. "This would never have happened in Philadelphia."

"Oh, now Harry," replied J.D., "I imagine there's a few good folks there too. Maybe you just haven't crossed trails with 'em yet. Not that I'd trade my home in Dust River Gulch for a place in Philadelphia myself, of course."

"I, uh . . . I, uh . . . can't believe it." Harry was lookin' down an' scratchin' his ears all a-puzzled.

Hare-Brain put his arm around his cousin, an' said gently, "I told you they was good folks, Harry."

Then, Rosie come over to Harry an' made a proposal. "We don't have enough to pay for ever'thing, only a little more than to pay for your damaged emotions. But if'n you'll give me a chance, I got some real good sasparilla soap, an' it's done a dandy job on tomater stains for me. Maybe I could try washin' your suit out for you."

Well somethin' musta' come over that ol' jackrabbit 'bout then. Like that first spring breeze comes blowin' over the prairie after a long, hard winter. It's warming down to the bone. Don't know if they's used to that out east or not, but 'round here in Dust River Gulch, it feels real familiar.

"Would you do that for me, Miss Rosie?" answered Harry softly, "And . . . about those damaged emotions—I think they're better now. You don't have to pay for them. As a matter of fact," Harry paused and looked over the crowded diner like he was addressin' a courtroom jury, "You don't have to pay for anything! Sheriff, rip up that lawsuit! I want every *whereas* and *wherefore* in your trash-bucket by noon."

"You've got my word on it, Harry!" said J.D., an' with that he walked right over an' hugged Rosie an' Harry together.

"That's the spirit," added Jack. "I just knew you'd come around after all."

"Guess it just runs in the family," said J.D. with a wink.

An' then there was just the greatest commotion you ever seen. They was a-hootin' an' a-hollerin' —everybody happy as a dog with two tails waggin'. Harry declared he'd stay awhile after all, an' dumped his travelin' money into the barrel along with all the rest.

"One thousand eight hunerd an' ninety-eight dollars," shouted Tumblewheeze, "an' thirty-seven cents."

"Yahoo," yelled Bo.

"It's all yours, Rosie," declared Harry and everybody agreed.

"Well I declare," added Rosie. "That should take care of a few repairs around here."

"I'll say," said Claude. "What you gonna do with the rest of it, Rosie?"

"Why I believe it'll make a nice dowry," replied Rosie, with a wink in J.D.'s direction.

"Yahoo!" Bo yelled. An' the party got goin' all over again. I think it lasted most all day an' on into the night— like a family reunion or some such thing.

Well, its jest like I said a while back, right? We're like family 'round here.

Oh yeah, you might be interested to know, that Harry, he ain't been back to Philadelphia yet. An' he wears that suit every time he an' Jack eat over at Rosie's place. Marvelous stuff, that sasparilla soap.

IN CONCERT
Miss Penelope Shetland
Sings all yer favorites an' more!

FRIDAY NIGHT

under the stars
at the Oakey-Doakey Corral
You ain't heard singin' till you heard this show pony!

CHAPTER TWO
High Notes

Ever notice how some things just ain't what they seem? Why even rightcheer in Dust River Gulch you can walk right down Main Street an' see all them two-story buildin's. There's the Dust River Gulch Hotel, Lefty's Five & Dime, the Dry Goods Store, even the Confectionery. Full two-story buildin's, every one—'cept of course they ain't really. All of 'em got a false front, with nothing more than an attic up top. Don't you sorta wonder why we done that? Maybe there's a touch of dishonesty in all of us. We's always hopin' to seem a little better to them folks who's just takin' a glance in our direction. But it don't matter to them who knows us ever' which way. You think we'd know better, wouldn't you?

Guess we all might better take a second look more often, cause like I said, things ain't always what they seem. Take that Doc Hardly, for example. Oh my, he weren't hardly no doctor after all! If'n it weren't for good ol' J.D., we might not of seen that fox for what he really were until it was too late. But I best not get all stirred up 'bout that all over again. My, oh my, still got two bottles of his elixir myself.

You know, I was just thinkin'. A perty song along with a perty face, why that can outdo even the most powerful elixir mostimes—'specially on menfolk with a tender heart. An' if a lady adds in a couple extra secret ingredients . . . well, that's powerful stuff! I reckon even the most sensible feller might let his good sense wander off with such a formula.

I was thinkin' about another pair of strangers that come by Dust River Gulch not so long ago. Entertainers by trade, 'least that Miss Shetland was—and how! She put on such a show, now didn't she? An' all to help out her poor ol' Papa. Apparently, they'd struck tough times along the trail. It was Sherriff Saddlesoap that come across 'em first just outside of town. Ol' Papa Shetland had one leg all bandaged up. He was limpin' along draggin' their baggage behind 'em. Meanwhiles, Miss Shetland had all she could carry too, an' bless her heart, she was singin' a sweet song to raise her poor lame Papa's spirits.

Oh don't you cry for me,
I come from Alabama with a bandage on my knee . . .

"Hello," called J.D. "Mighty sweet singin', Miss."

Miss Shetland looked up an' smiled, "Thank you kindly, sir. I didn't see you there." She blushed. "Look, Pa, it's a lawman."

Her pa barely looked up under his big straw hat. "What's that—a lemon, ya' say? I sure could use a tall glass of squeezed lemon."

"Not a lemon, Pa, a LAWman," replied the perty pony.

By then J.D. got the ol' feller's attention and introduced hisself, "Sheriff J.D. Saddlesoap, at your service," he said, tippin' his hat to the lady.

"The Sheriff!" Pa cackled with delight.

"Maybe our luck done changed for the better, Pa." Miss Shetland brushed her thick blonde mane back from her face.

"You had some trouble?" asked J.D.

At that, Miss Shetland shed near a cloudburst of tears. Her pa patted her gently, then he looked over to J.D., "Nothin' but trouble, Sheriff. Nothin' but trouble."

Miss Shetland wiped her eyes with a lacy hanky an' whimpered, "I'm sorry, Sheriff, it's been so hard takin' care of Pa. An' we's had nothin' but trouble along the trail."

"I'll be glad to help you if I can," replied J.D.

"Oh, would you, Sheriff?" an' that perty pony clutched onta J.D.'s hoof in gratitude.

"Well, uh, maybe we could start with a proper introduction," said J.D. "I'm Sheriff J.D. Saddle . . . uh, guess I done told you that."

"Penelope Shetland," she says, an' courtsied real lady-like, "*Miss* Penelope Shetland. An' this here's my Pa."

"Pleased to meet you, Sheriff Saddlesore."

"That's Saddlesoap," J.D. corrected him.

"Saddlesap?"

"SaddleSOAP, Pa," interrupted Miss Shetland, then flashin' a smile, she whispers to J.D., "Pa's a little hard of hearin'."

"Well let me help you with that baggage there, an' we'll head into town for some refreshment," says J.D.

"Why thank you, Sheriff," said Penelope, lettin' her eyelashes flutter like a butterfly. "Sure is fine to have a strong feller like you 'round."

J.D. gulped. He strapped all that luggage onto his back and turned toward town. "Just foller me," he added.

"Sure will," said Penelope. "Let's go, Pa!"

So the three of 'em come amblin' into town. When they got to Rosie's, J.D. plopped down their luggage outside, and held open the door.

"Thank you, Sheriff, I'm much obliged," said Penelope, brushing by.

Behind her, hobbled Pa Shetland takin' a whiff of those fine vittles in Rosie's kitchen. "Smells mighty good in here," he says.

So they all set down at a table an' waited to order. Now this particular day it weren't Tuesday, so I don't reckon there's much cause to praise Miss Rosie's tomater soup here. That's the Tuesday special, of course.

Instead, J.D. tells Rosie to cook up a mess of grits, covered in slumgullion, with fried cornbread on the side for the newcomers, addin' on that he'll pay for the order.

"Why thank you, Sheriff," says Penelope, a-pattin' J.D. on the shoulder.

"Ahem," Rosie starts a-clearin' her throat. "An' who might you be?" she says with a smile.

"Oh, yes, uh, Rosie," says J.D. standin' up like a shot, "this here's Miss Penelope Shetland an' her Pa."

An' they all gave their proper greetin's.

"An' what brings you all to Dust River Gulch?" asked Rosie.

"Well, Pa here's perty hungry right now," says Penelope. "Maybe you could run along an' get them vittles an' we can chat later, Miss . . . I'm sorry, what was your name again?"

"Rosie," she replies, and hustles herself off to the kitchen.

"Speakin' of names, Sheriff," Penelope starts in again, "I hope it wouldn't be too forward of me to call you J.D. . . . I mean, you been so kind."

"Oh, J.D.'s fine," replied the Sheriff.

"An' I do hope you can stay an' eat with us, . . . *J.D.*" Penelope twirled a bit of that blonde mane a' hers. "Wouldn't that be nice, Pa?"

"Ice? Yeah I'll have some ice."

Miss Shetland smiled, "Then we'll just have Miss What's-Her-Name get you some."

"That's Miss Rosie," J.D. said. "Uh, I suppose I could stay. Let me go order up some more chow meanwhiles."

"Oh, J.D., you don't hafta do that. I won't eat much anyways. You know a gal's got to watch her figure," said Penelope. "Why don't you just sit down an' join us?"

Well, the Sheriff, he sat back down. An' Penelope was as happy as a cat gone mousin'. Rosie, she brought the grub, just like she's s'posed to, an' it seemed like ever' time she passed by the table, Penelope had need of something for Rosie to fetch, like a napkin, an extry fork, a cup of tea. I tell you, that Miss Shetland, she sure kept Rosie busy. (Though you'd think she'd remember Rosie's name a little better, wouldn't you?) But she sure didn't have no trouble with J.D.'s name, what with her sayin' J.D. this, an' J.D. that, an' payin' him more attention than a heifer does grass. Meanwhile, Pa Shetland ate his fill, maybe more'n once.

An' Penelope kept on, "J.D., you must just be the bravest mustang I ever known."

"Well, uh . . ."

"An' I'm guessin' you're a music-lover to boot. Am I right, J.D.?"

"Miss Shetland, I . . ."

"Oh, J.D., why so formal?"

"P-Penelope . . ."

"Just Penny's fine with me, J.D."

"Penny, I don't want to give you the wrong impression."

"Oh, you can't fool me, J.D. I sure did appreciate your kind remarks when we first met, about my singin' I mean."

"Well, actually I . . ."

" 'Course if'n it weren't for my singin', ol' Pa and I'd be worse off yet."

"Worse off?"

"Why yes, J.D., what with Pa comin' up lame an' all, I don't know how we'd get by without my singin'."

"You mean you sing professional-like?"

"Why, J.D. Saddlesoap, you clever rascal! You done found me out!"

"Well . . ."

"Yes, I sung in my share of towns. Wish I didn't needta ask for money, but we's had such bad luck. Ain't that right, Pa?"

"Have a bite? Sure. If'n you don't want it, I'll eat it," answered Pa.

Then Sherriff J.D. had a notion come on him like a bolt of lightnin'. "Why, Miss Penelope," he began.

"Penny."

"Uh, Penny. We could have you sing for us rightcheer in Dust River Gulch!"

"Surely, you don't mean for money."

"Well, why not?" declared J.D. "This town's always lookin' for a fine talent like yours."

"Oh, J.D.!" Penelope squealed, a-throwin' her arms right around J.D.'s neck.

An' right then Rosie comes by with toast an' jam (for Miss Penelope, of course), an' wouldn't you know, it slipped right offa that tray and plopped right down on Miss Shetland's blonde, curly mane—jelly-side down.

"Oh, I'm so sorry!" said Rosie. "Let me help you clean that up." An' she took a napkin to it, but it just got all smeared around.

"Oh, that's all right, Posie," said Penelope, sorta talkin' through her teeth. "I'm sure you don't mean to be clumsy."

Well, J.D. he jumped up an' told Rosie the good news. "You'll never guess, Rosie, but Miss Penny here's agreed to put on a concert for all us here in Dust River Gulch. She's a professional singer."

"Miss Penny?" Rosie raised an eyebrow.

"Uh, Miss Shetland, here. An' Friday's the usual night for suchlike entertainment 'round town. Is that agreeable to you, Pen—er, Miss Shetland?"

"Anytime you say, J.D.," Penelope purred back best as a pony can.

"Well then it's all settled!" continued J.D., workin' up a sweat just talkin'. "An' Rosie, once I get these folks checked into the hotel next door, maybe you could take care of their meals for the next few days?"

"Anythin' you say, J.D." replied Rosie with her own kinda smile.

Then Pa Shetland piped up, "Did you say, dessert? Sure, I'll take some dessert!"

"I-I better go set things up at the hotel for you," said J.D., excusin' hisself. Penelope waved goodbye. Rosie just crossed her arms.

Then J.D., he stumbles on a chair, nearly fallin' over, but he makes his way to the door an' outta there like he's in some kinda hurry.

Well J.D. took care of business at the hotel an' got on with his reg'lar 'rounds in town. Things was perty quiet, 'ceptin' he kept thinkin' he heard Penelope singing softly somewheres. An' it was a mite distractin'.

Come and stay by my side if you love me,
do not hasten to bid me adeiu . . .

J.D. shook hisself and went on about his business.

"Sheriff J.D., you all right?"

J.D. looks down an' there's Bo the lizard right in fronta him.

"Sorry," answered J.D., straightenin' his kerchief. "Didn't see you there."

"Hmmm," Bo looked at him sorta sideways. "You sure you're all right?"

" 'Course, I'm fine," says J.D. "What can I do for you?"

"Well, I think you better come over to Rosie's 'fore Claude takes another hit from her fryin' pan."

"Uh-oh. He didn't go waterin' down no soup again, did he?"

"I don't reckon so. Maybe you just better come an' take a look-see."

"All right," J.D. agreed.

So off they went to Rosie's.

All the commotion was back in the kitchen. J.D., he cracked open the door just a bit to see what he was up against before steppin' into the middle of that argument. Rosie could be mighty feisty when she got riled.

"So just cause it looks sweet, you think you can go ahead an' taste it," she scolded.

"It weren't much," Claude whimpered, a-rubbin' his shaggy head, "just a spoonful of honey-custard."

"You fellers is all the same, ever' one of you." Rosie started again, "An' it ain't just custard. If it looks sweet, you can't resist it!"

"Well, I . . ."

"Well, supposin' it were poisoned or somethin'," said Rosie.

"Poisoned custard?"

" 'Course fellas never can tell that. Long as it looks sweet, they say, it's all right. Don't they, now?"

"Guess so." Claude didn't seem too sure.

"You's all the same—ever' one of you!" Rosie was a-rantin' like a full-force wind now, "*Looks* good, *smells* good, *sounds* good, must *be* good you say. Well, let me tell you. It takes a gal like me to see whether it's good for you or rotten to the core!"

"Sorry, Rosie, but it's just custard."

"That custard's spoken for—if that means anythin' to ya!" With that, Rosie shook her frying pan at Claude an' he bolted out the back door like he's fresh-branded.

Just outside the other door, Bo looked wide-eyed at J.D. an' whispered, "What were that all about?"

"I'm not absolute sure." J.D. swallered hard, "but it seemed like more'n honey-custard."

Just as the two bewildered fellas made their way across the dinin' room, who do you think comes in the front door? None other than Penelope, an' she's got herself all gussied-up in the fanciest dress you ever saw. You might say she was perty as a whole bowl of honey-custard.

"J.D.!" she squealed. "Why I declare! An' I was just comin' for supper. It sure is nice of you to join me. We got so much we need to talk about!"

"We do?"

"Why, we got to make all the arrangements for Friday night's concert!"

"I was thinkin' that you . . ."

"I can hardly wait to hear all your plans, J.D., but let's sit down first, shall we?"

"Well, I . . ."

"Rosanne, yoohoo! Where is that gal when you need her?"

Well, Rosie showed up just as Penelope was leading J.D. over to a table. "Here's one with a little privacy, J.D. Let's set a spell."

An' so it went again, but without Pa this time. He was back at the hotel with a bellyache.

Penelope did all the plannin', while J.D. agreed without sayin' more'n two words together. Meanwhile Rosie's bustlin' back an' forth waitin' on Miss Penelope, an' all the while lookin' crosswise at J.D. He figured if Rosie brought out that fryin' pan, he was headin' for the door lickety-split.

She didn't, but when it was time for dessert, he didn't dare ask for no honey-custard.

By the time dinner was done, ever'thin' was settled 'bout the concert. Tickets would start sellin' tomorrow. An' what a time it would be!

Well, Friday night the town was all a-bustle. Professional-like entertainment don't come our way too often, so near the whole town shows up—for fifty cents a ticket, even! 'Course there were a few notable exceptions. Ol' Gray Mary declared she didn't need no entertainin' what cost half a dollar. An' Pa Shetland weren't there neither. Rumor had it his bellyache come back, though he sure seemed fine at lunchtime. An' for some reason or 'nother, Rosie didn't show up. Wonder if'n it had to do with that concert poster sayin' that the music sung that night would be dedicated to Sheriff J.D. Saddlesoap. An' Miss Shetland, she had quite a program lined up. There was love songs, pop'lar tunes, even a touch of opera! An' it was all to be sung under the stars out at the Oakey-Doakey Corral. This was gonna be a night to remember. Wooowee!

Well, some fellers set up a hay wagon under the old oak tree by the edge of the corral. That was the stage. An' they was lanterns hangin' from the branches to light it all up. Ever'body else done gathered 'round in the corral, settin' on blankets or barrels or whatever they could muster.

At half past eight, J.D. stepped up onto the stage to introduce the star performer—Miss Penelope Shetland. An' if you thought she was gussied up the other night, then you ain't seen nothin' yet. Her golden mane was bundled up like a hornet's nest. An' the sleeves on her dress poofed out near's big as the puffball ol' Tumblewheeze McPhearson found out backa his woodpile a couple years back. She was some show pony!

After a considerable time of clappin' mixed in with hoots an' hollers, Miss Shetland started her performance.

"First off I'd like to thank Sherriff J.D., for his 'specially good treatment of me over the past few days, an' for makin' this whole concert come into bein'. J.D., don't know what I'd do without you." An' she blows him a kiss from the stage.

Then there was more cheerin' an' whistlin' whiles J.D. stands up for a minute. He looked 'bout as comfortable as if he's barefoot on a porcupine, but he waves to the crowd anyways.

Then Miss Penelope commenced singin' a love song:

In the sky the bright stars glittered.
On the grass the moonlight fell.
Hush'd the sound of daylight bustle.
Closed the pink-eyed pimpernel.
As a-down the moss grown wood path
Where the cattle love to roam.
From an August evenin' party,
I was seein' Nelly home.

Her voice passed over that crowd like a soft breeze off a fresh mown hayfield. They was spellbound. You coulda heard a chicken feather drop, 'cept for a sniffle here an' there. By the time she finished two more verses—each raisin' up more sentimentals than the last—we was all starin' at that stage like it were the only place worth seein' for miles. An' maybe it just was at that.

Then Miss Penelope went on to singin' about more broken hearts than you can shake a stick at—Genevieve's, Clementine's, you name it! An' she cast her same spell on that crowd with ever' one of them songs. Don't see how nobody could listen to that perty pony sing, an' think about anythin' else in the world.

But as matters were—back in town—Rosie had a lot on her own mind, don't you know. So she took herself a walk down Main Street. Looked like a ghost town, it did! But she was appreciatin' the quiet. Sometimes that's the best thang you can hear—nothin' at all. Specially when inside your head, your thoughts are shoutin' at you noisy as a hoedown. So though Rosie's heart mighta still been achin', at least her head was a'clearin—helped along by that peace an' quiet.

Ting, tinka, ting.

"Now what was that?" Rosie wondered. She looks around. "Don't see nothin'."

Scritch-scratch, tinka, ting.

"Hmmm," she cocks her head. "Sounds like it's a-comin from the Bank an' Trust."

So Rosie, she sneaks over near the front winder of the Dust River Gulch Bank and Trust to take a peek. An' whattaya think she sees? Why it looks like a burglar! An' he's comin' through the roof, then a'lowerin' hisself down a rope. Rosie pulls back 'round the corner a little more, still strainin' to see without that burglar seein' her.

Who is it? Why, it looks like it could be Pa Shetland's younger brother! Er, wait, it's Pa Shetland hisself—but he's got no bandage on his leg, his gray whiskers is gone, too, an' he's not wearin' that old straw hat no more. Pa Shetland was no old pony. He was a strappin' young mustang!

If Pa Shetland weren't what he seemed, then where's that leave Miss Penelope? Rosie figured it was time to get J.D.! So she snuck off to the corral at the edge of town.

An' that's where we left Miss Penelope, ain't it? Singin' like a sweet mournin' dove. By now she's moved on to some fancy opry tune.

I am a maiden, cold and stately,
Heartless I, with a face divine,
What does I do with a heart innately?
Ev'ry heart I meets is mine!

Meanwhiles, Rosie was working her way through the crowd, lookin' all around. "He must be up front," she says to herself.

Folks was whisperin', "Move away. Cain't see!"

Rosie just clenched her jaw an' kept movin' toward the front, where J.D. sat by the haywagon stage.

"Rosie!" J.D. was surprised to see her sidled up next to him. "I'm glad you come. This Miss Pen . . . er, Miss Shetland here, she's real good!"

"Actually, J.D., she's real bad!"

"Oh, now Rosie, I know she's a flirt, but cain't you just enjoy her singin'?" whispered J.D. back.

"J.D., you gotta come down to the Bank an' Trust. Her *Pa* is down there robbin' it."

"What?!"

"You heard right, . . . an' I expect her *Pa* can hear just fine too, by the way. You git down there an' you'll see what I'm talkin' about."

"If you say so, Rosie."

"I'll stay here an' keep an eye on Miss Penelope," says Rosie, clenchin' her hooves.

Well just then, Miss Shetland finished up her opry tune, an' the crowd stood up a-roarin' with applause. "Thank you all so much." She smiled an' courtsied. Then it seemed she saw Rosie in J.D.'s place an' the Sheriff a-workin' his way back 'round the crowd away from the stage.

"Oh, Sherriff Saddlesoap," she called. "You cain't leave yet! This next song's dedicated special to you, J.D." An' she fluttered them eyelashes somethin' fierce.

"Stick around, Sheriff," called out some feller in the audience.

"Yeah, Sheriff," said another, an' several folks grabbed holda him to keep him there. I imagine they wanted to hear that song.

"I'm sure your little errand to town can wait awhile, J.D.," called out Penelope.

"That's right," agreed the audience.

Then Rosie, she spoke right out, "Who said he's goin' to town, Miss Shetland?"

Penelope paused, then answered, "Well, I just assumed."

"Maybe he's just goin' to get me some refreshment," Rosie answered with a swagger in her voice. "Let him go," she calls back.

Well at that, J.D. broke loose from the crowd an' started back toward town at a gallop. As you can imagine folks started a-murmurin', wondrin' why Rosie's makin' such a fuss.

But she weren't done, not hardly! She stomps right up onto that stage an' face to face with Miss Penelope. An' that Rosie, her nostrils were flarin'. Claude done seen that look before.

"Now, Miss Penelope, maybe you'd like to tell ever'body here what your dear ol' *Pa's* doin' tonight," Rosie challenged.

Suddenly Miss Penelope's smile weren't so sweet. But she gave it another try, "Why, poor Pa's feelin' poorly, tonight. But I think he'd want us to get on with the show with or without him." She turned to the audience. "Don't ya'll think so?"

An' that brought on a smatterin' of clappin' an' suchlike. Then Rosie bellered out, "Maybe your Pa can come over after he finishes emptyin' out the Bank an' Trust?"

Well, that set off all kinds a commotion in that there corral. Miss Penelope backed away from Rosie; she looked ever' which way. Folks was crowdin' 'round the haywagon.

That cornered pony took herself a deep, deep breath—suckin' air like a blacksmith's bellows—then she faced toward town an' let out such a shriek. Now I reckon you mighta heard a train whistle right by your eardrum one time er 'nother. You mighta even'a heard a tornader or two—like that one what picked up Curly Armadillo's barn last spring an' thumped it upside-down in the middle of Main Street. But you ain't never heard nothin' so loud as Miss Penelope's shriekin' cry.

"PAAAAAAAAAAAA-BLOOOOOOOH!" she wailed.

At that high-pitched shriek, ever'one of the lanterns hangin' nearby shattered like they been hit by buckshot, plungin' the whole place into natural darkness. Folk's ears was ringin' like noontime bells on the fourth of July. I tell you, the whole corral was stirred up like a chicken house with two foxes an' a 'coon. At the center of it all, the hay wagon rocked and creaked, splinters a-flyin'. I don't rightly know what happened. It were too dark to see it, but by the time somebody got another lantern lit, it was quite a sight.

There on that stage was Miss Penelope Shetland—hogtied and disheveled. Her dress was tattered, even her poofy sleeves done went flat as flapjacks on the griddle. An' that blonde hair that'd been piled high as a hornet's nest, looked to me like them hornets come back an' ransacked the place. She even had hair stuffed in her mouth!

Rosie, she looked a little winded herself, but she called out, "Don't just stand there a'starin'! Git down to the Bank an' help J.D.!"

So some strappin' townfolks did just that. An' 'fore you know it, here comes J.D. with the whole posse draggin' that thievin' mustang, *Pa,* along with 'em. Or should I say *Pablo Shetland?*

"Caught him red-handed," said J.D., "cleaning ever' bit of cash outta the safe. Guess he was too busy to pay attention when she called out his name. Not that it weren't loud enough, Miss Shetland." J.D. paused, seeing her hogtied on the hay wagon. "Hmm, looks like you took care of business here, eh, Rosie?"

"My pleasure," says Rosie, pushin' some of her own red hair back in place. "Miss Shetland might of charmed ever'-body else in town, but she didn't fool me."

J.D., he just shook his head.

"Guess she had to keep you occupied," says Rosie, "whiles her partner's scopin' out the robbery."

"Sorry, Rosie, you had 'em pegged. It looks like I'll be eatin' crow for some time," replied J.D., humble as I ever seen him.

"Looks like it," agreed Rosie. "But when you're done, I got a whole pot of honey-custard for you!" An' with that Rosie flashed that smile that's reserved for J.D. alone.

"Rosie," says J.D., "you're the greatest!"

SHERIFF J.D. SADDLESOAP
AN'
MISS ROSIE
invite you to their

WEDDIN'

an' garden party afterwards
SATURDAY MORNIN'
in the cactus garden of
MR. AN' MRS. CURLY ARMADILLO
Main Street, Dust River Gulch

CHAPTER THREE
Windy Wedding

You know, we always loves a party 'round here in Dust River Gulch. An' a weddin' party to boot. Well there ain't none better than that! 'Specially when the marryin' couple done been through a lot together, like J.D. an' Rosie been.

Maybe you heard say that "love conquers all," but that don't mean it ain't a little battle-worn first. In fact, my guess is, that makes it stronger yet. Any blacksmith worth his salt knows you don't forge good tools in a small flame. You gotta sweat a while. An' let me tell you that J.D., he did his share of sweatin' when Miss Penelope was in town, now didn't he? Guess that made the rope a little stronger when he an' Rosie tied the knot at last.

Anyway, like I said, we do love a good weddin' party. An' what a party was planned! Mrs. Skunk, Cyrus' wife, lent out her cactus garden behind their place for all the festivities. An' this time of year they's all a-flowerin'—looked like a big outdoor boo-kay . . . Texas-size! That cactus garden was Mrs. Skunk's pride an' joy. She sure knew how to grow 'em. (Most folks waters 'em too much, she says.)

"Hope them blooms an' blossoms hold out till weddin' day," Mrs. Skunk says to Cyrus. "We's towards the end of the season by now."

"Ahh, don't fret your head about it, Emma Jean," says Cyrus. "It'll be fine."

"This just happens to be the biggest weddin' in these parts for a month of Sundays, an' it's happenin' rightcheer in my own backyard cactus garden, Cyrus," replied Mrs. Skunk, with the hair on the backa her neck raisin' up. "Somebody better fret a little. If'n it ain't your concern, I guess it better be mine!"

"Emma Jean, you'd worry 'bout whether the sun's comin' up, if you was up early enough."

"Cyrus Skunk! Just what are you insinuatin' by that remark?"

Well, might be best if we leave the Skunks to tend to their own business for now, an' get on with the rest of the preparations. Like say, the vittles? Why all the womenfolk in town was a-fixin' 'em. Near as good as the county fair. Ever'body's makin' their prize recipes, tryin' to outdo the other. First off, ol' Gray Mary was makin' the weddin' cake. Guess she'd earned the right for that honor by old age alone. Hear tell it'll be seven layers thick! Curly's wife, "Q" as her friends call her, fixed up some of her famous twister macaroni quiltin' bee supreme. (Don't know how she crochets them noodles.) An' you ain't never had pickles like the ones Miss Bovine makes—her double blue-ribbon watermelon pickles canned by the barrel are hard to beat. An' I cain't forget to mention the pumpkin Indian loaf with molasses sauce that Dixie McPhearson whips up. That'll stick to your ribs ('most ever'thin' else along the way will too.) Mmmmmm, there's just nothin' like a weddin' party with all the fixin's!

An' then there's the fancy duds too. There was boots to polish, spurs to sharpen, an' tuxeder's to let out—Texas tuxeders, that is—consistin' of a white shirt, black vest, string tie, an' your best dungarees. An' hats—ten-gallon, twenty-gallon—the bigger the better! Then you start on the ladies. They's sewin' more hoops in their skirts than a jackrabbit could jump through. Puttin' wildflowers into their best hats, settin' out white gloves, lacy kerchiefs—you name it! Cain't help but wonder where they keeps all this stuff the rest of the time. An' how about that clever Q Armadillo? Heard tell she made Curly's coonskin cap into a parasol!

Rosie declared she didn't need more'n a simple white dress, but the womenfolk, they wouldn't have none of it! Nothin' but the best. So they quit their reg'lar quiltin' bee for two months just to make her a fancy weddin' dress. An' her train was near as long as the Cannonball Express itself!

Maybe by now you got the proper notion—this weddin' would be somethin' grand! It seemed ever'body was so busy with all the fixin's, they hardly had time for nothin' else. Bo the lizard, J.D.'s best man for the weddin', got so busy he didn't even floss his teeth for a week. Now that's what I call busy! Busy, busy, busy. Busy like a beaver at a waterfall, I tell you.

With all this goin' on, J.D. started missin' Rosie's company. Seemed like he barely saw her. She'd be called off from the restaurant to check the guest list (ever'body), pick a photographer (I think she went with that Mr. Brady from outta town), look at the menu for the party, an' I don't know what-all else.

So the day before the weddin', J.D. thought he'd try again, just to spend a little time with Rosie. So off he goes to the restaurant about lunchtime. When he gets there, Claude's runnin' around like his britches is on fire, tryin' to keep up with all the customers in the place.

"Workin' the place by yourself again, Claude?" said J.D., a mite dissappointed.

" 'Fraid so, J.D. Rosie's off for a final fittin' for that weddin' dress."

"Well, she's hard to come by nowadays."

"You can say that again," answered Claude, headin' off to another table. "Be with you soon as I can, J.D."

"Never mind, Claude," J.D. calls back. "I'm gonna go hunt down Rosie."

So J.D. gets up from his table, an' the feller from the next table grabs holda his vest to stop him. It's Tumblewheeze McPhearson.

"What you doin' 'Wheeze?" asks J.D.

"I gotta stop you, Sheriff," the dusty ol' weasel replies.

"Stop me from what?"

"Why, goin' to see Rosie, of course."

"Now you tell me one good reason I cain't go see Rosie, 'Wheeze."

" 'Cause it'd be bad luck. There's your reason."

"Bad luck?"

"You cain't see your bride in her weddin' dress afore the weddin' itself. Like I said, it's bad luck!"

"I ain't seen her to say more than howdy do for pert' near a week now!"

"Well now sure ain't the time. That's for sure. An' another thing . . ." started the weasel.

So J.D. heaved a sigh an' set hisself down at Tumblewheeze's table, next hearin' how he'd best get a new broomstick for the weddin' too, if'n he knew what was good for him.

"Now why do I need a new broomstick?" asked J.D. "The weddin's outside."

"Heh, heh, it ain't for sweepin', J.D. You got to jump over it!" Tumblewheeze leaned back in his chair and laughed some more. "Sweepin'—heh, heh." Then he leans over to the feller at the next table. "Did you hear that? J.D. thought he'd be sweepin' with a new broomstick on his weddin' day!"

"Oh, hoo, ho, ho, ho," laughed that ol' feller, his belly shakin' like a loose barn-board in a stiff breeze. "Sheriff, you just beat all. Hoo, ho, ho."

"No weddin's complete without the couple's jumpin' over a new broomstick, J.D. Why it'd be downright improper."

Just then Claude shows up for the order.

"Gimme some of Rosie's tomater soup," says J.D., a'shakin' his head. "Guess that's the closest I'll be gettin' to her for today."

After lunch, J.D. mosied on back toward his office. Along the way, Bo come tearin' 'round the corner in a cloud of dust. Ooof! He runs smack into J.D. there in the street an' papers flies outta his arms ever'where.

"You all right, partner?" asks J.D. helpin' him up.

The lizard rubs his nose a mite, "Think I'll make it. . . . But can you help me gather up these papers?"

"Sure," says J.D., lookin' over a few as he picks 'em up. "Why, Bo, these is all sheet music."

"Yep, got to git them over to Miss Bovine," Bo replied. "She'll be pickin' one to sing for your weddin'."

J.D. raised an eyebrow, "Bo, you ever heard Miss Bovine sing before?"

"Don't look at me," says Bo. "She insisted. Why, I might be pickled along with one of her watermelons if'n I told her she cain't sing at the weddin'."

J.D. nodded, "She does take pride in her ability to beller it out. Guess we cain't git in her way."

"No sir, not me!" Bo agreed.

"Just do me a favor then," added J.D. "Just ask her not to sing this one." An' J.D. shows Bo the music for "When I Saw Sweet Nelly Home." "It might bring back some unpleasant mem'ries."

"She'll never see it." Bo took it and wadded it up in his pocket.

So J.D. headed on down the street, an' weren't it a-bustlin'? It was downright precarious! He had to dodge a load a pickle barrels that come rollin' offa the back of one wagon. Then here come four burly fellers totin' a player piano down the street, an' some gal fussin' along behind 'em at every step. Next J.D. had to duck his head under Mrs. McPhearson's trellis bein' carried right down the middle of the street. An' they was all headin' for the Skunks' backyard where there's a jam-up like you wouldn't believe! J.D. thought he'd best stay outta the way till mornin'. So he did.

Next mornin' the weather started out hot, an' it got hotter. Hotter than the topside of a desert rattler. 'Fore long, it were downright swelterin'! But at the Skunks' place, things were still movin' at a fever pitch.

"This heat sure ain't gonna help that ice sculpture none," said Emma Jean, moppin' her brow. "An' how we gonna keep the punch cool?"

"Least it'll be wet," said Cyrus.

"Oooh, Cyrus, cain't you at least—"

Emma Jean was interrupted by a knock at the door, so she hustled on over.

"Mornin' Mizz Skunk."

"Mornin' Jack."

"Where'd you want me to put this here carrot punch," says Hare-Brain, peerin' from behind a big black kettle.

"Oh, there it is. Just put it out back in the cactus garden, between the player piano an' the seven-layer weddin' cake. No, wait. Maybe you better keep it under the trellis for now, outta the sun."

"That's where I put them pickle barrels," called out Cyrus.

"Guess I better go look myself," then says Emma Jean. "Come on through, Jack, but watch your step."

So Mrs. Skunk led Hare-Brain Jack, a-luggin' that kettle of punch through the house 'round casserole dishes, polished boots, music stands, and I don't know what all. Just when he gits out the back door to the garden, he hears Emma Jean let out a scream just ahead of him. Well that jackrabbit jumped an' hadta handle that big kettle of punch like a master-juggler till Cyrus rushed over to help him set it down in the path, spillin' no more'n a drop or two. "What's the matter, Emma Jean?" yells Cyrus. "Nearly spilled the whole kettle of punch!"

"It's the cactus blooms, Cyrus," she says, white as a sheet. "They's . . . they's turnin' brown around the edges!"

"Well, for cryin' out loud, Emma Jean," sighed Cyrus. "Is that all?"

"Is that all?" squealed Mrs. Skunk, an' the hair started raisin' on her back.

"Why I noticed that this mornin' 'fore you got up. That's when I watered 'em."

"You what?"

"You heard me, I watered 'em, an' it's a good thing I did, too, let me tell you, or they'd be brown through to the core!"

"Whadda YOU know about cactus blossoms?"

Well at that point, Jack excused himself politely and hightailed it outta there, though I couldn't say that them skunks noticed him leavin'. They was well into their spat by now. An' as you might guess, things went from bad to worse. They weren't done till they'd raised such a stink there in that cactus garden like you never smelled before! An' just in time for the weddin' guests to arrive an' all.

So here they come, all prim an' proper. Then that smell hits 'em. You shoulda seen the faces them folks made. Oooooweee! Miss Bovine took on a look like a muskox, an' I think Curly's hair even straightened out at that smell. But they didn't dare say nothin', now did they? I did notice a good number of ladies with their kerchiefs to their noses, though. An' they was fannin' somethin' fierce, just hopin' for a breeze.

Up to the front stepped ol' Judge Parsons, his mustache a-twitchin. Then out struts J.D. in his Sunday best. He cut a fine figure, even though he was sweatin' like a pig. An' Bo's standin' there by him, fumblin' in his pocket for a hanky or anythin' to block that scent. Then the piano starts crankin' out a real sweet tune. An' Miss Bovine, she began a-bellerin' out a love song, an' I reckon it'd be enough to chase even Gruffle O'Buffalo back to the prairie.

"Cyrus," Emma Jean whispers, "roll out the red carpet!"

"I's about to, Emma Jean!" replied the surly skunk.

Then down the middle aisle it comes, unravelin', unravelin', unravelin' till the end of the carpet flops down at Rosie's feet. She's a-waitin' there at the back, an' lookin' as much like a fairy tale princess as we ever seen in these parts. An' you know what? A fresh breeze come blowin' through just then. Guess that awful smell couldn't stick around no longer—not when that sweet Rose made her entrance. An' I'd say at the sight of Rosie, nobody hardly heard Miss Bovine's bellerin' no more.

By the time Rosie reached the front, the wind had really picked up. Rosie's long white veil started flappin' in the breeze, an' soon it nearly covered over all the folks a-settin' on the front row. Havin' finished her song, Miss Bovine unraveled the veil, bunched it up and sat down on all the extry. Then ever'body could see J.D. an' Rosie, their hair blowin' in the wind, standin' side by side before ol' Judge Parsons. An' that sure did churn up the mem'ries of them townfolk.

Why think back to all the times them two saved the day together. Why the folks of Dust River Gulch couldn't be more grateful—an' now it all come to this. My, oh my! Well the ladies did their share of sighin, an' a good bit of cryin'. Ain't that always the way?

But the wind kept a-whistlin'. Miss Bovine's sheet music done picked up an' left. Before you know it, Emma Jean lost her hat. If'n it hadn't blown into Dixie's molasses sauce, why, it mighta' blown clear to the next county! Ever'body started holdin' things down—'specially them that had hooped skirts. Then the trellis started swayin' with every gust. Curly an' Tumblewheeze roped it down, bein' as quiet as they could so's not to disturb the proceedin's.

"Psst, 'Wheeze," Curly nudged the weasel, "how much longer you reckon Judge Parsons'll take to get them two hitched?"

"Better not be long," Tumblewheeze whispered back. "I think I see a dust cloud a'comin' this way . . . just yonder."

'Fore Curly turned his head, that whirlwind was already spewin' dust all through the weddin' party. The wind got even stronger. It blew off the top layer of that seven-layer weddin' cake right into the carrot punch. It flipped up the red carpet an' flopped it over the trellis. Soon fancy hats an' cactus blossoms were a-flyin' all through the garden! The wind were so loud, them folks couldn't even hear ol' Judge Parsons no more.

The wind caught under Q Armadillo's parasol an' lifted her right outta her seat, blowin' her into Miss Bovine's lap! Poor Bo's hat did near the same for him. That whirlwind caught under the brim, an' he was flyin' 'round in circles like a jayhawk on a string. Lucky for him, he caught hold of the player piano on one pass.

"Don't know if'n we can hold on much longer, Judge Parsons," called out Tumblewheeze, near chokin' on the dust. "Better tie the knot quick!"

Well, no sooner than he said it, the wind, it died back down. Through the dust cloud them folks heard the ol' judge's pronouncement.

"Ladies and Gents, let me present to you . . . Mr. an' Mrs. J.D. Saddlesoap."

Well at that, ever'body got to clappin'. They clapped an' cheered till the dust settled 'round an' they could see the smilin' newlyweds come outta the cloud.

Bo gave the player piano a crank, an' started up the music. Then folks throwed rice like it was plantin' time as the Saddlesoaps come marchin' down the middle aisle. Of course they had to step over hats an' flowers, a couple layers of cake an' even what 'peared to be a brand new broomstick along the way. "Guess it's official, now," said Tumblewheeze with a satisfied snort.

"Now let's eat!" says one or two fellers, with gen'ral agreement.

But them vittles hadn't weathered the dust storm too well. There weren't more'n two layers of that seven-layer cake together anywheres. Mrs. Armadillo's twister macaroni quiltin' bee supreme done come untied in that whirlwind. An' the pumpkin Indian loaf with molasses sauce had collected a good bit a dust, not to mention sev'ral articles of clothin'. But safe inside them barrels, one thing was good as ever. That's right. Miss Bovine's double blue-ribbon watermelon pickles! An' you know what? I reckon that was enough.

Yeah, there was quite a mess at that party. Sometimes all the fixin's just gets in the way, don't they? Got to step over 'em an' around 'em just to get to the good part. 'Cause J.D. an' Rosie, they was still as happy as two lovebirds in a tree. An' I do believe since then, Cyrus an' Emma Jean cleaned up their house an' home too. Saw 'em just a week or so ago, out workin' together in their flowerin' cactus garden. Now, ain't that somethin'?

CHAPTER FOUR
Ghost Town

Can't rightly explain it, but things was perty quiet whiles J.D. an' Rosie was gone honeymoonin', an' we was right thankful for that. 'Specially since Bo the lizard was named deputy for then.

Now don't git me wrong, I got nothin' agin' Bo. He's a fine feller an' all, but not much of an imposin' figure. Why, he ain't more'n two foot tall—not countin' his tail. Don't think he could of stood up to any considerable-size outlaw. You might remember how Gruffle O'Buffalo nearly blew him down jest by breathin' in his direction. An' of course, Bo ain't the brightest coal in the campfire neither, but he does have spunk, an' I guess that's why he was left in charge.

Bo did keep busy. Let's see, there was the spat that broke out twixt Cyrus an' Curly—somethin' about Curly's coonskin cap that come up missin'. An' somebody got in a snit about Miss Bovine's disturbin' the peace with her singin' practice. That was a delicate situation. But there weren't no real trouble while J.D. an' Rosie were gone. Nothin' we couldn't work out ourselves.

Even so, Bo was countin' the days till J.D. got back. He even marked the day on his calendar—the seventeenth of the month—an' it was J.D.'s birthday to boot! Sure hoped he could hold out that long.

Now meanwhiles, them two newlyweds had been doin' a heap of travelin', let me tell you—went clear outta the county! J.D. an' Rosie had been to visit the sites, ever'where from Klondike Kanyon to Possum Trot Pass. Guess they'd seen ever'whar worth the seein'. But even then I'll bet they was feelin' homesick for good ol' Dust River Gulch, don't you reckon? There's no place quite like it—'specially when it's home, sweet home. So right on schedule, back they came.

The stagecoach dropped 'em off at their house near the edge of town. An' the place was peaceful as a fiddle with no strings. Nobody's there to greet 'em. Didn't see a soul.

"Let's walk into town, Rosie," suggested J.D. "Maybe they all forgot we was comin' back today."

"Could be," said Rosie, "Let's go see ever'body." An' off they ambled toward Main Street.

Now it weren't much past noon. On most days Dust River Gulch would have been hummin' like a reg'lar bee-hive at that time of day. But when the Saddlesoaps come amblin' into town, whaddya' think they seen? Pert' near nothin'! The place looked like a ghost town!

"Well, I'll be," said J.D. "Whar is ever'body?"

"Looks like they all packed up an' left," exclaimed Rosie. "What coulda' happened, J.D.?"

"Don't rightly know." J.D. shook his head. He looked this way. He looked that way. Not a soul!

"Let's try the Dry Goods store," suggested Rosie. "Maybe Tumblewheeze or Dixie can tell us what's up."

"Tumblewheeze'll know," J.D. smiled.

So the two of 'em headed into McPhearson's store. When the door squeaked open all they could hear was the echo.

"Hey, 'Wheeze, we's back!" called out the Sheriff. No answer.

"Dixie!" called out Rosie.

Nothin' but the wind a'blowin'.

They peered 'round the counter an' saw the Mason jars full of beef jerky, bear bacon bits, an' a dozen other mouth-waterin' treats—but no McPhearsons. They stepped into the back room. The walls were draped with buckskin pants, bandanas, bloomers, an' petticoats. But they was all empty.

"Hmmm. Not a bad price on these bloomers," said Rosie, checkin' the tag.

"Not now," said J.D. "Let's go find some folks somewhar first."

So they headed on over to the Confectionery across the street. But there weren't nobody there neither.

"Funny thing is," said J.D. walkin' 'round the counter, "this fudge looks fresh." He scooped himself a hoof full. "Tastes fresh, too." He was about to take another hoof full.

"Now, J.D.," Rosie reminded him, "not now."

"You're right," replied J.D., backin' away from the fudge. "Let's go find some folks first."

They walked back out into the empty street.

"J.D., whatta you reckon's goin' on 'round here?"

"Wish I could say, Rosie. Looks like Dust River Gulch's done been deserted."

"You mean it's become a ghost town?"

"Sure seems like it," J.D. scratched his chin, "an' near overnight, too."

"Well I'll be . . ."

"Wait." J.D. stopped, twitched his ears, an' turned around. "You hear that, Rosie?"

"What?"

"Thought I heard some pitter-pat or somethin'."

"I didn't hear nothin'."

So they kept on a'walkin'. But their ears was perked like a pot of coffee, an' eyes peeled like Vidalia onions.

After no more'n a minute, J.D. turned—sudden as a weathervane in a whirlwind.

"Rosie," he says, "looky there."

"I don't see nothin'."

"That little dust cloud by the corner of the Post Office, I'll go check it out."

So J.D., he snuck back, quiet as a drop of molasses, to peer 'round that corner.

"See anythin', J.D.?"

"Nope," he called back, "but I sure am gettin' suspicious." Rosie held his arm as they continued walkin'. J.D., he was keepin' a real close eye ever' which way he could. As they passed the Livery, J.D. wheeled 'round again.

Splash!

"What was that?" cried Rosie.

"I don't know what, but I got a notion of where to look for it!" J.D. stomped over to the waterin' trough, an' whatta you think he seen?

"Bo?!"

Yep, there's that lizard, sunk down in the waterin' trough holdin' his breath. So J.D. pulled him out, "Get outta there afore you drown yourself!"

Bo sputtered an' spattered. He coughed a few times. Then he looks up at J.D. an' smiles kindly, "Welcome back, J.D.," he says. "You too, Rosie." He tipped his hat as the water poured out. "Um, uh, . . . powerful hot weather, ain't it? Ooooowee! Nothin' like a cool dip in the trough to cool a feller down."

J.D. raised his eyebrow. He put his hooves on his hips.

"Uh, you look mighty hot, too, Sheriff. . . . Can I gitcha a drink?" Bo dipped his hat in the waterin' trough an' offered it to J.D.

"No thanks," replied J.D. "Maybe you can just tell me whar ever'body is."

"Whar they is, eh?" Bo squeezed out his kerchief. "You mean the townfolk?"

"Mighty quiet 'round here, don'tcha think?"

"Now that you mention it, it is mighty quiet," replied Bo. "So, uh, why don't we all head over to your place, Rosie?"

"It should be closed today," answered Rosie. " 'Fore we left, Claude told me he had some other business to tend to this week."

"Then why's there smoke comin' from your kitchen stovepipe?" asked J.D., a'peerin' down the street towards Rosie's restaurant.

"Uh, could be to take the chill off," said Bo, quiverin'. "Brrrrr! Turned a little nippy now, didn't it?"

J.D. just glanced sideways to Rosie. "Let's go check it out."

"I'm with you," she says.

"Oh, me too," added Bo. "Just a-headin' there, myself."

Well, strange as Bo was actin', J.D. an' Rosie didn't have time to ask any more questions. They was headed for the restaurant lickety-split. Like they say, "Where's there's smoke, there's fire," and like they might add, "Where there's fire, somebody done lit the stove!"

So they comes up close, an' sure 'nuff there's smoke comin' outta the stovepipe at the back.

"Shhh!" whispers J.D., "Think I hear somebody in there."

"I'll go in an' check it out for ya, Sheriff," volunteers Bo, an' he starts for the front door.

Well, J.D. grabbed him an' yanked him back, "Git back here, Bo. That's too dangerous! You an' Rosie guard the front door. I'll sneak 'round back."

"Oooh, uh, O.K., J.D."

So J.D. began sneakin' his way back 'round the buildin'. An' he had to go a good ways, with several buildin's connected side-to-side there in town. Once he was out of sight, Bo started a-frettin'. "Oh dear me."

"What's the matter, Bo?"

"I done messed up this whole thing."

"What thing?"

"The surprise party, Rosie, for J.D.'s birthday."

"Dear me, Bo. I didn't know you was plannin' a surprise party!"

"Now J.D.'s gonna burst in an' surprise ever'body from the backside!"

"Maybe I can head 'im off at the pass," said Rosie. She turned to follow in J.D.'s path an' stopped short. She had quite a startle! Here comes another lizard just about Bo's size walkin' down the middle of Main Street!

"Jed?" Bo gulped.

"Bo! Is that you, cousin?" asked the approachin' lizard.

"Jed! It's me," called back Bo. "But what you doin' here all the way from Lonesome County, Idaho you ol' buckaroo you?"

"Haw, haw," laughed Jed. "Ain't you the joker, Bo? You knew I was a-comin' for my birthday visit today—just like my letter said."

Well at that, Bo started a-sweatin' an' squirmin' in his boots. You see, he'd been so busy bein' deputy whiles J.D. was gone, an' what with all the fixin's for this here surprise party for J.D., he plum forgot all about his cousin Jed's own birthday, an' his comin' to visit to boot! Now what was he gonna do? It's bad enough to mess up one birthday, let alone two on the same day! I tell ya, he felt about as low as the bellybutton on an earthworm.

Now Rosie, she sensed trouble, so she took things into her own hand. She slipped into the front door of the restaurant. She shushed ever'body powerful-like 'fore they got half of their "Surprise!" out. Whiles ever'body's still a-wondrin' what for, Rosie told 'em all to sit tight. Then she went through the kitchen to the back door an' gave J.D. a whistle.

"All clear," she says to him, then pulls him right in, "but we got ourselves another kind of emergency." Meanwhile she's pullin' her apron off the hook and tyin' it on.

"Is anybody in here?" asked J.D.

"Oh, yeah," says Rosie. "Ever'body's in here." Meanwhile she's pullin' her cake decoratin' tools outta the drawer.

"Ever'body?" J.D. scratched his head.

"I'll explain it all to you later, but for now, why don't you go back 'round to the front door an' keep Bo an' his cousin busy till we're ready."

"Cousin? Ready for what?" asked J.D.

"You'll see soon enough, but you better git goin' now."

Well J.D. hardly knew what to think. But bein' a newly-wed an' all, he reckoned he'd better go along with Rosie's plan. So he hustled out the back door, an' 'round to the front again.

There was Bo, still squirmin' in his boots, though he sure seemed glad to see his cousin all the same. J.D. trotted up an' gave hisself a proper introduction.

"So, Jed, what brings you all the way to these parts?" asked J.D.

"Why, it's my birthday visit," answered the visitor, slappin' Bo on the back. "My cousin here always has such a grand celebration for me on my birthday that I wouldn't miss it for the world."

"You don't say?" J.D. smiled, "Ain't that somethin'? Today is my birthday too!"

"If that don't beat all!" laughed Jed. "Think of that, Bo."

Bo managed a measly smile. Them two birthdays was a weighin' on him like a heavy burden by now. If J.D.'s surprise was ruined that'd be bad enough, but if'n it weren't — now that might be even worse! Jest think how Jed would feel left out if the only birthday party in town weren't for him! An' he come all the way from Lonesome County, Idaho, too. Bo wished he could just slither down between the cracks in the boardwalk an' disappear. He leaned against the front door, an' felt lower than a bellybutton on an earthworm who'd been swallered by a mole that fell into a well. Then, "Aaaargh!" backwards Bo fell, right into the doorway of Rosie's.

"Surprise!" yelled a whole dining room full of folks. "Happy Birthday!"

The place was all fixed up like a reg'lar hoedown! There was streamers an' balloons. Folks was a-wearin' party hats like they was a bunch of clowns. You'da thought the circus come to town!

"Happy Birthday, Jed!" called out Rosie as she came out from the kitchen carryin' a great big birthday cake. At that ol' Bo squeaked his finger in his ear. "It sure sounded like she said *Jed,*" he thought to hisself. "Musta' fell down too hard."

But when Bo looked at that birthday cake, he couldn't hardly believe his eyes, scrawled out in thick red frostin' was the message, "Happy Birthday, JeD! Welcome Buckeroo!" Though it looked like a couple of words had a little doctorin' done to 'em.

Jed smiled, an' wiped a little tear from his eye. "Bo, you're the best cousin a lizard could ask for!"

Rosie, she just looked down at Bo an' gave him a wink.

Then that there birthday party got as fun as a-jumpin' on Gramma's feather bed! Tumblewheeze got out his fiddle an' they all started a promenade. When they got hot, they stopped for some of Jack an' Harry's famous carrot-ice. Then they started up again.

An' Jed . . . he was so appreciatin' of it all. He was really surprised at gettin' presents from folks who hardly knew him. Shiny new spurs, nearly the size of his boots! And a

vest—big enough to camp out in! Them folks sure were generous. An' to think that his own cousin thought so much of him to set it all up! He couldn't hardly thank him enough.

'Course you might wonder where this all left J.D. Weren't it his birthday too? Well, it sure was. An' he declared it was his best one ever.

DUST RIVER GULCH'S 1ST EVER
BASEBALL GAME

for the gen'ral enjoyment of the community

SATURDAY

at the Oakey-Doakey playin' field

COME CHEER FOR OUR TEAM!

Pitcher- Sheriff J.D. Coach/Catcher- Harry

1ST Base- Claude 2ND Base- Jack

3RD Base- Tumblewheeze Outfield- Bo, Curly, Cyrus

CHAPTER FIVE
Off Base

Well I reckon it's that broken winder that started it all. Funny how an interruption to your plans can twist ever'thing around like that. J.D. was a-settin' in his office makin' a plan for how to make use of the Oakey-Doakey Corral—an' havin' quite a struggle with the decision.

You see, ol' Smiley Crenshaw, the owner of the place, had moved on to San Francisco. Seems his brother, Horace, done struck it rich away out there. He come into a heap of money on some claim of his, an' he invited Smiley to come out an' help him spend it in high style. Well Smiley decided he'd do it, an' havin' no more need of the corral he gave it over to the town of Dust River Gulch for the "gen'ral enjoyment of the community," as he put it.

So J.D. was settin' there, puzzlin' about the best use of that property. He figured that usin' it as just a corral weren't very enjoyable for the townfolks. Times past it'd been used for special events, like that famous rodeo 'twixt Gruffle O'Buffalo an' Sheriff J.D. hisself. Reckon the townfolks had enjoyed that show, but it sure gave J.D. a stiff neck an' a sore belly. Maybe more rodeos weren't such a good idea. Then how about for outdoor concerts? Why, they could bring in professional singers an' . . . Hmmm, maybe not. He recollected how Miss Penelope Shetland had brought all that trouble along with her concert. He got the notion that Rosie might not take kindly to another singer comin' to town for quite some time. Well then, what could it be? J.D. scratched his chin.

Ker-SMASH! Tinkle, tink. Through his winder it come crashin'. "I declare!" J.D. exclaimed, jumpin' right outta his chair, "What was that?" An' whatever it was rolled right under his desk.

"Dear me, Sheriff!" come someone callin' from outside, "You all right?"

"I reckon," replied J.D, "Is that you Harry?"

"Yes sir, an' I'm so sorry," Harry, Jack's cousin, come runnin' in. "Don't worry, I'll pay for the damage."

"You mean I don't have to file a lawsuit?" J.D. smirked.

"You're never goin' to let me live that down, are you, Sheriff?" Harry shook his head an' smiled back.

"Maybe if you promise me you won't move back to Philadelphia," J.D. answered. (Guess he'd grown fond of Harry by now.) Then J.D. bent over an' picked up what come crashin' through his winder. It was little round sack, all stitched up with red stitches, an' inside was somethin' hard as a walnut. J.D. looked at it kinda sideways, "Reckon this sack is yours, Harry."

"Sorry, J.D. Thank you. . . . Did you say 'sack'?"

"It's a curious little sack, Harry. What you got in there? It's packed up tighter than an Injun drum."

"J.D., you mean you've never seen a baseball?"

"Baseball?"

"Why everybody's playin' it back east. I got this ball sent to me from . . ."

"Wait, let me guess," J.D. interrupted him, "it's from Philadelphia, right?"

"Now this baseball's not just some eastern thing, J.D. Folks are formin' baseball teams all over the country."

"You mean it takes a team to open that thing up?"

Well at that Harry laughed so hard he nearly popped a button on his fine suit. "You don't open a baseball, you play with it—nine fellas on a team, against another nine fellas."

"Now your pullin' my leg, Harry. Eighteen fellers all playin' with a little stitched up sack all at once? Don't they got nothin' better to do?"

"J.D., baseball's played on a big field, with bases all set up like a diamond. One fella throws the ball, another fella hits it with a bat, an' then he runs around the bases."

"Well if that don't beat all. You mean they throw this little sack an' beat it with a stick? No wonder it's all stitched up!"

Harry couldn't hardly stop laughin'. "I've just got to show you how to play, Sheriff. Why we can get ourselves a team up right here in Dust River Gulch! There's nothin' better for the community's general enjoyment than playin' baseball."

"Did you say 'gen'ral enjoyment'?" asked J.D.

"Sure," answered Harry.

"Sounds good to me! Let's go rassle up a few fellers from town, head down to the Oakey-Doakey Corral an' try ourselves a game of this here baseball," said J.D. with a satisfied snort.

An' with that J.D. an' Harry headed down to Rosie's restaurant to round up some of the reg'lars. Let me tell you, that baseball sure did arouse some curiosity. Nobody'd ever played a game like that (they were more partial to horseshoes in Dust River Gulch), but some said they'd heard of it. Most said they'd like to give it a try, except for one ol' goat who said he wouldn't go runnin' in circles chasin' a little leather bag if'n they paid him a million dollars! But they got plenty enough fellers for a team or two, an' out they all headed to the corral, tossin' 'round that baseball along the way.

Well, when the group got out to the Oakey-Doakey playin' field ('cause that's what it was now), Harry showed 'em all how to set up a proper baseball diamond. They used burlap sacks of pataters for the bases, an' half a bale of hay for the pitcher's mound. They poured paint down the baselines, an' raked up the infield.

"So far, this ain't much fun." murmured Cyrus Skunk, workin' on the stripes.

"You can say that again," answered Curly, wipin' the sweat offa his face, "I coulda plowed my own field in the time I'm done rakin' this one."

But Harry assured them that they was nearly done, an' he was right. Then he commenced explainin' the rules of this here game, called baseball. He told about strikes an' balls.

Bo scratched his head. "Are you sayin' that ball ain't really a ball if'n it's a strike?"

"That's right," said Harry.

"Still looks like the same thing it were last time," said Bo. "How come you keep changin' its name?"

Harry just went on. He told 'em where to stand in the batter's box.

"Don't see why you'd wanta stand in a box of batter," muttered Claude, "that stuff can git mighty gooey!"

When Harry talked about stealin' bases, ever'body looked in J.D.'s direction. Guess they figured if'n they dared to steal anythin' they'd have to answer to him. Harry went on. By the time he got to the part about sacrificin' flies, them fellers was startin' to wonder just what they got themselves into.

"How long we gonna play this game?" asked Tumblewheeze.

"Nine innings," answered Harry.

"Oh, I cain't stay out that late," answered the weasel, "I got to be in by seven."

"Baseball's not measured by time," said Harry, "Like they say, 'It ain't over till the fat lady sings.'"

"Is he talkin' 'bout Miss Bovine?" whispered Cyrus over to Bo.

"I hope not," answered the lizard.

Well by now Harry got the notion that it might be best just to start up playin' an' let 'em all learn as they went. So he just called out, "Play ball!" an' the first ever baseball game in Dust River Gulch commenced.

On account of his fine horseshoe pitchin' skills, J.D. was named the pitcher. Claude played first base, Hare-Brain Jack took second base, and Tumblewheeze was at third. Harry sent Bo to the outfield, and put Cyrus Skunk behind home plate to catch.

"All right, Curly," says Harry. "You're up to bat."

So the pudgy armadillo picked up his rake, and mosied over towards home plate.

"An' try your best to hit the ball," Harry reminded him.

So J.D. wound up an' tossed the ball right toward the plate—nice an' easy.

Curly swung that rake with all his might, but missed the ball by a country mile. The ball plopped right into Cyrus' paw untouched. Then *BLAM!* Curly brought that rake down with all the might he could muster—right onto the ball— with Cyrus still holdin' it.

"Oowwwww!" yelled the skunk, droppin' that ball like it were a hot patater. Off bounced that ball, an' Curly right after it slammin' down his rake time after time.

"I got it again!" shouted Curly all worked up to a fever pitch. "Got it! Got it! Got it!"

Well by now Cyrus was perty near done seein' stars an' he took off after Curly like a shot. He grabbed the rake outta his hand an' broke it over his knee, *snap,* just like that! 'Fore you knowed it, they was rollin' 'round in a cloud a dust like a tangled-up tumbleweed, or should I say stinkweed? My oh my!

Well, once the other fellers got 'em untangled, Harry set the rule straight, "You're only supposed to swing at the ball in the air, Curly—just once." Well Curly, he was mighty sorry, let me tell you, vowed he'd git it right next time. But Harry thought it best if Curly an' Cyrus played in the

outfield for a while till the air cleared, so he sent 'em out—
way out—one to the right an' the other to the left. Then
findin' no other volunteers, Harry took over at catcher.

"Bo, why don't you come up to bat next?" he offers.

So Bo, he did. He grabbed half-a Curly's rake handle and
stepped into the batter's box.

"Choke up a little, Bo," suggested Harry.

Well Bo looked back, raised an eyebrow, then cleared his
throat best he could, "Ahemm!" He pounded on his throat
an' coughed.

"Are you all right, Bo?" asked Harry.

"Sorry, I cain't oblige you, Harry," said the lizard, "I got
nothin' to choke on."

Harry rolled his eyes. "That's all right. Just take a good
swing at that ball," he said, then added, "in the air."

"I'll do my best," answered the lizard.

Then J.D. stooped over an' pitched that ball, slow an' low
to the ground. Low enough to shave a caterpillar.

Ol' Bo swung at that baseball like he was about to chop
down a tree in one stroke! You could hear the wind behind
that swing, let me tell you, an' what do you know? He hit
it—full force!

THWACK!

The baseball jolted off the rake handle like a . . . like a
. . . well, it were sorta like a box turtle on a slow day. Went
about three feet.

"Run!" shouts Harry right behind the plate. Well that
scared Bo enough so he did. He went a-runnin' off in
Tumblewheeze's direction lickety-split.

"Other way!" shouted the weasel, standin' on third base.
"Go for first!"

Wide-eyed as a bullfrog, Bo headed toward Jack at second. Jack shook his head an' pointed toward Claude. Bo
turned right an' headed for first. He ran so fast his hat blew

off. He turned 'round an' picked it up, then headed off again even faster.

Meanwhile, Harry picked up the ball an' tossed it in Claude's direction. Bo glanced over his shoulder an' he saw that ball comin' up behind him, it was gainin', gainin', then it passed over his shoulder. So Bo put hisself into a whole 'nother gear an' beat that ball to the first base bag by no more'n a chicken's whisker.

"Safe!" shouted Harry, an' there was a twinkle in his eye as he says to hisself, "Now that fella is fast! With a little more baseball smarts, Bo might be able to play the whole outfield by himself."

Well, the team worked all afternoon gettin' them "baseball smarts." After a few more hours of practice—you know what? That team weren't lookin' too bad! 'Fore the shade of the old oak tree had stretched across the field, Harry congratulated 'em all an' said, "Why you fellas might even be ready for a little competition." An' just maybe they were at that.

Well, by Saturday, that team was runnin' like a well-oiled cotton gin. They all headed over to practice that mornin' at Oakey-Doakey field, an' a good number of townfolks come to watch 'em, too. Rumor had it that another team would be comin' to town that day, comin' to challenge the home team. Nobody'd want to miss that!

While the rest of the team was warmin' up, Harry was struttin' 'round, talkin' to all the players, "Way to get the ball over the plate, J.D.! That's right, Curly, good swing. Nice catch, Cyrus. Good throw, Bo." They was lookin' perty good, let me tell you.

Judge Parsons had been readin' up on the rules of the game, an' reckoned he could be umpire for the game. Dixie McPhearson said she'd keep score best she could. Miss Bovine declared she'd sing the anthem at the start.

Ever'body had a share in makin' this game of baseball a real source of enjoyment for the community.

J.D. felt real good about how ever'thin' seemed to be workin' out just fine. Guess it was worth a broken winder after all, eh? As you might guess, though, when things seems a little too good to be true, they prob'ly is—an' they were about to take a turn for the worse.

J.D. made a pitch, just like any other—straight over the plate. Cyrus was battin'. He popped the ball up, way up in the air betwixt the pitcher's mound an' third base. Both J.D. an' Tumblewheeze went scramblin to catch it, strainin' their eyes, lookin' up into the sun. Guess they didn't even see one 'nother.

Ka-Blam! They collided an' fell together in a heap there on the infield. J.D. tumbled onto Tumblewheeze, an' the ball dropped right on J.D.'s head. *Boink!* He was out cold.

When J.D. opened his eyes, he found hisself under the shade of the old oak tree with Rosie at his side.

"J.D., you all right?"

Things still seemed a mite foggy, but J.D. answered, "I reckon."

"Think you can play?"

"I reckon," J.D. stood up an' brushed hisself off.

Then Rosie called out, "Hey fellers, J.D. says he can play!"

Well that brought on a heap of cheers, hoots an' hollers.

"Good thing," added Bo, " 'specially with Tumblewheeze out."

"Tumblewheeze out?" J.D. puzzled.

The ol' weasel rolled up his pant leg to show J.D. a big white bandage wrapped all over his knee, "Cain't play," he answered, "My knee's swoll up like a toad a'croakin'."

"Sorry, Tumblewheeze," J.D. said, shakin' his head. Then he started to wonder, "So who's gonna play third base?"

At that, Rosie replied, "You're lookin' at her!"

"You, Rosie?" asked J.D., "but you ain't . . ."

Just then from over by home plate, Judge Parsons calls out, "Play ball!" So the team started over to the field before J.D. even finished.

"Sure glad you're gonna pitch," said Claude, with gen'ral agreement.

" 'Cause we sure are gonna need you," said Harry.

"You can say that ag'in," nodded Hare-Brain Jack, "You ain't gonna believe that other team!"

"Oooowee! That's right! Better believe it!" added the others.

So J.D. takes a good look over towards the field for his-self. "Cain't be!" he says, a'rubbin' his eyes, 'cause who's he see warmin' up on the pitchers' mound? None other'n Snake-Eye Smith, that rascally rattler he done dueled with way back when. An' who's on first? That's right—it's Doc Hardly, that elixir peddlin' menace! An' second base, if it ain't Billy the Kid, I'll eat my hat. (If he don't eat it first!) An' what a troublesome mountain goat he was at that. Third base, Pablo "Pa" Shetland, lookin' fit as any mustang you ever seen. Then at shortstop, there's the Buzzard-Breath Kid flappin' around. Lookin' back in the outfield, J.D. saw Cactus Face Curt, an' lo an' behold, a couple of bum steers to boot. J.D. reckoned where there's bum steers, there's gotta' be . . . an' there he was, back behind home plate. The other team's catcher was none other than—you guessed it— that mangy heap of buffalo-hide hisself, Gruffle O'Buffalo!

Well J.D. couldn't hardly believe his eyes, His head was spinnin' like a fresh-sprung tornader. "How did all them villains git outta' prison an' on this team?"

"While you were out cold, Judge Parsons said somethin' about some new prison recreation program, J.D.," answered Harry, commencin' with his lawyer's explanation. "Apparently they got a lawyer who discovered a writ of *sine animo revertendi* and on the prisoners' behalf sued *ex statuto* for *de bono et malo en ex turpi causa*."

"What are you talkin' about?" answered J.D., "Can you tell me in English?"

But before Harry could translate it, Judge Parsons called out, "Play ball!" an' the outlaws got ready to bat.

Then Gruffle laid eyes on Sheriff J.D., "Well, if 'n it ain't the Sheriff?" he snorted. "Nice you could wake up in time for the game!" An' at that them two bum steers started a' snickerin' like they do.

"Good to see you agin', Sheriff. Ain't you had enough sleep lately?" asked Doc Hardly, with a smirk. Then Snake-Eye Smith laid his head on his rattle-tail an' pretended to snore, an' that set the whole gang of villains to laughin' all over ag'in.

"We'll just let our playin' do the talkin'." J.D. reminded his own team.

"That's right," agreed Harry. "We can beat 'em fair an' square."

"But I git the feelin' they ain't gonna play that way," said Claude, with gen'ral agreement.

"That may be their way," said J.D., "But we ain't gonna stoop to it."

An' with that, the baseball pride of Dust River Gulch took their places on the field (with Rosie substitutin' at third base) an' the game got started with J.D.'s first pitch. Snake-Eye Smith was up to bat. Here come the ball.

"High. Ball one," called out Judge Parsons.

Next pitch J.D. tried to git the ball lower—down in the snake's strike zone.

"High. Ball two," came the call.

So J.D. pitched the ball so low, it come just rollin' over the plate in the dust.

"Low. Ball three."

"What's the matter, Sheriff?" bellered Gruffle, "Still got sleepin' sand in your eyes?" an' that started up all manner of snickers, hoots an' hollers.

"C'mon, J.D." calls out Emma Jean an' some other town-folks started in.

"Yeah, you can do it."

"Strike 'im out, J.D."

Harry threw the ball back to the mound again. J.D., he scratched his chin. That snake was so low to the ground there weren't hardly no place to throw it for a strike. He pitched again.

"Ball four," called the Judge.

So Snake-Eye raised hisself up, tossed down the bat, an' sauntered off to first base—walkin' by loopin' one coil after another, an' smilin' to show ever' one of his crooked fangs. All this to the great appreciation of the other villains.

Next up was Billy the Kid. That Billy Goat was snortin', an' pawin' at the ground, just waitin' for the pitch. J.D. wound up to deliver the ball—straight down the middle.

Ker-Rack! Billy hit that ball right back so hard an' fast, J.D. had to jump over it. The ball plowed right through that hay mound an' bounced over second base before Jack could lay a hand on it.

Meanwhile, Snake-Eye bounded over to second base, whiles Billy charged at first like he'd butt Claude right offa' the base an' into right field. Somehow Claude avoided him an' managed to catch the throw from Bo, but just a little late.

"Safe at first an' second," said the umpire-judge.

"Two on, nobody out!" calls out Doc Hardly, "Looks like it could be a long pitchin' day for you, Sheriff! Just let me know if you need some elixer tonight. Hee, hee." Well, it did turn into a mighty long inning, an' it was just the first! Gruff hit a grand slam an' the villains' team had scored six runs before the Gulch team even got up to bat.

Rosie, bein' the only lady, she went first.

As she stepped into the batter's box, Gruff commenced talkin', hopin' to break her powers of concentration. "Hey, looky here, they got gals on their team. Ain't you got business back in the kitchen? Ooohh, think I smell your biscuits burnin'." An' that started up them bum steers somethin' fierce.

Rosie, she tried not to mind. Meanwhiles, Snake-Eye Smith went through more gyrations than a cowpuncher's lasso 'fore he finally pitched that baseball. When he did, that ball spun like a top through the air. It looped way off to the right, then took a turn for the left quicker than a New York politician. It came back 'round so hard, it made Rosie duck for cover. "Strike One," called the Judge.

Gruffle nearly laughed his scraggly mane off. "What's the matter, gal? Cain't take a curveball? Easy out, Snake-Eye, easy out!" he taunted.

Rosie bit her lip, then stepped back to get a better grip 'fore the next pitch.

Here come that curveball again. Rosie stepped right into it an' swung the bat.

Crack! She hit the ball high an' long. Way long, way back to the fence!

Runnin' back like a one-cow stampede, a bum steer jumped up an' reached back over the fence an' caught the ball on the tip of his glove. Then he come crashin' down on toppa' the fence, breakin' through the boards, landin' in a cloud of dust. But wouldn't you know it, he held on to the ball.

"Sorry, Rosie, but you're out," said the judge.

Rosie took a squinty-eyed glance at Gruff on her way back to the dugout, a-clenchin' her hooves.

Then Bo comes up to bat. "So you're bringin' out the big guns?" chuckled Gruffle O"Buffalo, standin' like a mountain over the little lizard.

Bo just stepped up an' waited for the pitch.

Just as the snake delivered the ball, Gruff let out a cough so strong it nearly knocked Bo off his feet.

"Strike one," came the call.

Bo stepped back into the box.

Here come the pitch, right down the middle. Here come the cough on the backa' his neck.

But somehow Bo got some wood on that ball, an' it dribbled out four feet in fronta' home plate.

Gruff jumped up to fetch it, Bo shot towards first 'fore he got stepped on. An' quick as a wink, that lizard was on base before Gruff got the ball outta' his glove.

The townfolks cheered like nobody's business.

Then up comes J.D. to bat.

Snake-Eye starts his big wind-up. *Whoop-tee, whoop-tee, whoop.* Here it comes.

J.D. takes a swing so hard, it turns him 'round like a corkscrew.

"Strike one."

"Oh, Sheriff," starts in Gruff, "that was quite a breeze. Can you fan me some more?"

Next pitch. Another swing an' a miss.

"That breeze is gettin' downright chilly now," says Gruff, pretendin' to shiver. An' that got them steers a'goin'.

Whoop-tee, whoop-tee, whoop. The ball come flyin' straight at J.D.'s head. He dived for the dirt. Gruff stood up an' caught the ball.

"Ball one," called the judge.

"Careful now, Snake-Eye," called Gruff to the mound, "We don't want the poor Sheriff to hurt his head again, now do we?"

Ever'body from the villain's team said, "No siree" or "Cain't have that." Then they all started laughin' again.

They were still laughin' until J.D. hit the next pitch. *Pow!* The ball dropped just past Pablo, the third baseman. J.D. went tearin' off for first base before the outfielder figured out where the ball was. Meanwhiles, Bo set off like a lightnin' bolt. At second base he turned for third. He ran around third base, holdin' his hat. He turned for home base licketysplit. But uh-oh, look who's blockin' his way—that mountain of buffalo hide hisself—Gruffle O'Buffalo! But Bo, he saw a clear path betwixt Gruff's legs an' he sprang for it. Bo passed under the shadow an' out to the other side, landin' in a heap on that sack of pataters.

"Safe!" come the call.

At that the big buffalo rocked backwards an' landed right on Bo's back. *Ker-Splat!* Bo found himself buried betwixt mangy buffalo hide an' a sack full of mashed pataters. One run was in an' J.D. was still a'comin' 'round the diamond. Doc Hardly tried to trip him at first. J.D. jumped. Billy tried to butt him at second. J.D. dodged. Pablo tried to tackle him at third. J.D. twisted around an' squirmed outta' reach. Then he headed for home base.

The outfielder finally found the ball an' tossed it to Gruffle a'settin' on home plate. The one ton buffalo snagged the ball in his mitt. He swung it around to tag the chargin' Sheriff.

Ka-THUD! J.D. hit that buffalo hide an' the whole play was lost in a cloud of dust.

When J.D. opened his eyes, he found hisself lyin' under the shade of the old oak tree with Rosie settin' by his side.

"J.D., you all right? That's the second hit to your head today!"

Things still seemed a mite foggy, but J.D. answered, "I reckon I'll get over it."

He rubbed his head an' looked around, "Where's all them outlaws?"

"Herded back to prison." answered Rosie, "Some lawyer showed up. Harry says he had a stay of *sinus revertimundo,* or some such thing."

"Sounds painful."

"It ain't a sickness, J.D. It's some sort of legal gyration. When Judge Parsons read it, he stopped the game and sent them villains back where they came from. They had to forfeit the game."

"Is that so?" J.D. sat up a bit, "an' what was that call when I . . ."

"J.D., don't you think that's enough about baseball for now?" Rosie said softly, "You better rest a while longer. I'll go get you some cool lemonade." So off she went.

J.D., he propped hisself against the old oak tree, just starin' out towards home plate . . . a'thinkin'. And before the dust clouds cleared from his head, he called out like an umpire, "Safe!" Then with a smile an' a satisfied snort he says to hisself, "Safe! Take that, you mangy outlaw."

After that, J.D., he felt fit as a fiddle at a barn dance. An' he never did ask again about that call at the plate.

I'd say when you give your best effort an' play by the rules, I guess the rest don't really matter that much, does it?

CHAPTER SIX

The Great Train Robbery

You might think I could go on forever tellin' one story after another about the good folks of Dust River Gulch. 'Course if I start tellin' the same ones all over again, just maybe I could at that! At my age, I sometimes have a hard time recollectin' where I left off one an' started up another. Ain't that somethin'? Then again—come to think of it— some stories get better the second or third time around, now don't they?

But this here story—well, that's somethin' else again. Cain't say I like the tellin' too much, but I reckon you oughtta know it. Guess it's the last story I got to tell about Dust River Gulch.

As you might figure, it all starts one particular mornin' at Rosie's Restaurant. Folks was a-slurpin' down their first cup of coffee whiles Claude was servin' up one order after another of that Dust River Gulch favorite—hominy grits an' eggs with gooseberry muffins smothered in blackjack molasses. Ain't nothin' better for breakfast! I tell you, with that dish, every part brings out the best in the other. Mmmmm-mmmm!

So when Rosie run outta' eggs—well that caused quite a stir!

"Why, you can't eat the breakfast special without eggs," declared Tumblewheeze, "It's all outta' whack!"

"You can say that again," added Bo, sittin' at the same table.

"Sorry, 'Wheeze," said Claude, "but Rosie says we's plumb out of 'em."

"Outta' eggs?" exclaimed the weasel. "Ain't Jack's chickens layin' no more?"

"Oh them chickens is layin' just fine, but with them rail-workers nearby . . ."

"Railworkers?" Tumblewheeze perked up his ears, an' peered up at Claude over his spectacles. You see, that ol' weasel made it his business to know ever'thin' that was goin' on in those parts—an' before Claude said that word, he hadn't heard nothin' about no railworkers. "What rail-workers?"

"Them fellers layin' track out east of town—'parently they's been buyin' lots of eggs from Jack lately. Workin' fellers do git hungry, you know."

"Well I'll be," exclaimed Tumblewheeze. "Layin' track, you say?"

"Yep," said Claude.

"An' buyin' eggs, you say?" added Bo.

"Yep."

"Well ain't that somethin'?" said both Bo an' Tumblewheeze together.

"So what you fellers want for breakfast then?" asked Claude.

"Uh, never mind," answered 'Wheeze. "I think I'd better get over to the store." An' the weasel set right out.

Claude scratched his head. "How 'bout you, Bo?"

"Uh, not now, thanks," answered Bo. "I got a notion to head out to Jack's place. See you later!" An' off he goes too.

Well once Tumblewheeze got past the front door, he set out a-runnin'. He scrambled down the street to his Dry Goods store. An' he come in a'pantin'.

"Dixie!"

"What is it, Tumble-honey?"

"You sent in that order for next month yet?"

"Here it is. I was just ready to run it down to the Post Office."

Tumblewheeze snatched the letter right outta her hand, tore open the envelope, an' started scratchin' out numbers an' scribblin' in new ones right then an' there.

"What's got inta you?" asked Dixie. "Why you changin' ever'thin'? I did it just like we always do."

"I'm doublin' it!" Tumblewheeze looked up for a second, "No . . . triplin' it!" An' he commenced a-scratchin an' scribblin' somethin' fierce again.

"Triplin'?!" Dixie exclaimed, "You gone crazy? We'll never sell that much stuff!"

"You better believe we will," answered Tumblewheeze, then he looked at her with a twinkle in his eye. "Dixie, the train's comin' to Dust River Gulch!"

"You're kiddin'."

"Nope, they's layin' track out east of town."

"Oh, Tumble-honey!" she squealed, givin' him a big hug. "Looks like we're in for some good business ahead."

"You can bet on that," smiled the ol' weasel. "Once the train stops here in Dust River Gulch—this here Dry Goods store will be a reg'lar gold mine!"

Then them two weasels went back to scratchin' an' scribblin' out their new order, sure that they was gonna sell ever' bit, an' maybe more.

Meanwhile, ol' Bo made his way out to Hare-Brain Jack's farm on the outskirts of town.

"Mornin', Jack!"

"Mornin', Bo. What brings you out this way?"

"Well, hmmm. I heard you was sellin' a whole lotta' eggs lately."

"Sure am."

"Well, you see, I was sorta wantin' to git into the egg business myself."

"You lay eggs, Bo?"

"Me? Oh no, not me—Ha! What I mean is—I want to do like you do, Jack."

"You mean you want to be my competition?" asked the jackrabbit, narrowin' his eyes.

"Well . . . I . . ."

Jack suddenly smiled. "Then you're welcome to try it! Lately, my hens can't hardly keep up anyhow. I think Dust River Gulch is big enough for two egg farms."

"Well thank you kindly, Jack. So then, uh, how do I start?"

"I reckon you can start with the chicken or the egg," answered Jack.

Bo scratched his head. "Now there's a tough question. Which should come first? Whatta' you think, Jack?"

"You got a chicken house?"

"Not yet."

"Then I reckon you better start with the egg," suggested Jack. "Tell you what, Bo—since you're a friend an' all—I'll sell you a whole dozen for half price."

"Oh thank you kindly, Jack. Thank you, thank you." So Jack pulled twelve fresh eggs out from under one of his best hens, an' put 'em in a sack for Bo. Then that lizard paid the price, an' started struttin' back toward town. Now he was in business! OoooWee!

"An' don't forget to keep 'em good an' warm," called Jack after him.

"Let's see," Bo muttered to hisself. "I got twelve eggs. They hatches into twelve hens. Then each of them twelve hens lays a dozen eggs each, an' they hatches into a dozen more hens. Hmmm, let's see—how many's that? Twelve plus one dozen a dozen times over plus another . . . then he yells out real sudden-like, "Yippeee! Coyote-Aye! I'll have eggs comin' outta' my ears in no time!" An' with that he set out a-runnin'. Sure hope he didn't crack none.

Well, it weren't more'n a few days before word was gettin' all around town—the train was comin' to Dust River Gulch! An' my how that news set things all a-bustle. You could see it was makin' changes all down Main Street. First off, McPhearsons added an extry room to the back of their

Dry Goods store. An' 'fore you knew it there was more hammerin' goin' on than a pack a woodpeckers on a dry stump. Ever'body was a-buildin' on, a-sprucin' up, all gettin' ready for them crowds of new folks that would be comin' once the train stopped in town. An' them railworkers—they was gettin' closer by the hour. Soon they was past Jack's farm, then two days later at the edge of town. By a couple of weeks or so, they done gone on by an' were workin' out in the western prairie on the other side. But behind 'em, they left them two shiny silver rails—an' to them townfolks, they was good as gold.

Back at Rosie's diner, them tracks was all folks could talk about, mostly. "I reckon they'll be sendin' the first train down the line any day now," said Tumblewheeze.

"You think them rails is finished all ready?" asked Claude.

"Don't need em' finished all the way," answered Tumblewheeze. "They can git to Dust River Gulch just fine all ready."

"I reckon they stretch all the way to Klondike Kanyon by now," added J.D.

"Could be," Tumblewheeze shrugged. "All I know is we better be ready 'round here."

"For them crowds you mean?" asked Claude.

"Sure!" snorted 'Wheeze. "An' I think you outta' reconsider my proposal, Sheriff."

J.D. rolled his eyes. "You gotta' bring that up again?"

"Well, you gotta think ahead, Sheriff! That Main Street's just too narrow!" says Tumblewheeze, bristlin' a mite. "I say we gotta make it wider!"

"But that means movin' all them buildin's!" J.D. protested.

"Gotta make way for progress, Sheriff!" Tumblewheeze crossed his arms. "Dust River Gulch ain't a fittin' place for no sticks in the mud."

"He's got a point there, J.D."

"Yeah."

"Think about it, Sheriff."

J.D. stood up. "How about we wait at least till the first train shows up?"

Tumblewheeze shook his head an' muttered, "Stick in the mud, I tell you. Stick in the mud."

J.D. walked out to the street, shakin' his head, wonderin' which side of the street the folks wanted to move. Most likely ever'body'd say the other side from where they was.

He walked 'round a ladder. Curly was at the top of it a-doctorin' up his store's sign.

J.D. read it, "*Confectionery World.* What was the matter with plain ol' *Confectionery?*"

"Gotta think big, J.D.," called down the paint-splattered armadillo.

"Guess you gotta keep up with the Dust River Gulch Hotel an' Resort Center," said J.D.

"Yep," Curly chuckled.

J.D. just shook his head, "At least Rosie's is still just a restaurant," he said to hisself.

When he got past the Dust River Gulch Bank an' Trust an' Worldwide Financial Services buildin', J.D. reckoned he'd better go pay Bo a visit.

"J.D.! Am I ever glad you come!" Bo cried out from his chair when J.D. opened his door.

"Good to see you too, Bo," J.D. greets him. "What you been doin' with yourself? Ain't seen you 'round town much lately."

"Guess you could say I been settin' around here at home mosta' the time," answered Bo.

J.D. looked at the lizard sideways. "Bo, why you got hay in your chair?"

"Well, glad you asked," answered Bo. "This here's my nest."

"Your what?"

"My nest. Uh, you see, I'm hatchin' up some chickens."

"Bo, why are you hatchin' chickens?"

"That's my business, J.D."

"Well then excuse me for askin'."

"No. I mean I'm in the egg business now," the lizard smiled, brimmin' with pride, "Gonna' make myself big money sellin' to them railworkers."

J.D. raised an eyebrow. "I hates to tell you this, Bo, but them railworkers is workin' in the next county."

Bo's jaw dropped open, "You're kiddin' me!"

"They been gone for days all ready. Prob'ly past Klondike Kanyon by now."

Bo, he started to fidget, "Well if that don't beat all. What am I s'posed to do with the hunerd an' forty-four thousand eggs I got under way?"

J.D.'s eyes got big as a full harvest moon, "Bo, don't tell me you're settin' on a hunerd 'n' forty-four thousand eggs!"

"No, 'course not," replied Bo. "Might as well be though."

"How's that?"

"Well, here's how I got it ciphered out, J.D. I'm settin' on a dozen rightcheer. They hatches into twelve hens. Then eacha' them twelve hens lays a dozen eggs each, an' they hatches into a dozen more hens. So that makes twelve plus one dozen a dozen times over plus another two dozen twelve times over an' that comes out to one hunerd an' forty-four thousand. . . . An' I had plenty of time to check my math on that too."

"I reckon you have, Bo. I reckon you have."

"Well," Bo scratched his scrawny head, "once the train stops in town, they'll be plenty of folks needin' eggs."

"Oh yeah, that train," nodded J.D. "Guess it's gonna make this into a reg'lar boom town, now ain't it?" He rolled his eyes. "Give me a holler when your chicks are hatched," says J.D. on his way outta' the door.

Well J.D. didn't have to wait long. By the next mornin' them twelve fuzzy little chicks was peepin' all over Bo's house. They was a-peckin' at his piggy bank, an' scramblin' under the bed, a-scratchin at ever'thin' in sight.

Sheriff J.D. stopped by to offer his congratulations. "Anythin' I can git for you, Bo—you ol' mother hen, you?"

"Yeah," Bo confessed. "There is one thing. Could you git me a newspaper? Actually, maybe five er' six of 'em while you're at it."

"No problem," says J.D.

"An' hurry up, if you don't mind."

"I understand," J.D. answered. So off he went to the office of *The Dust River Gulch Gossip Gazette . . . and World Reporter.*

J.D. bought a handful of papers an' headed back to Bo's place on the double. But on the way, he couldn't help but notice the headline, "Trains on Track by Independence Day!"

For that whole month till then, them townfolks nearly drove J.D. crazy. They was preparin' a celebration like you never seen before in Dust River Gulch! Emma Jean planned a parade down Main Street, featurin' flowered-cactus floats shaped like—well, you guessed it—a train engine, coal car, an' caboose. She figured the ladies' quiltin' bee society should make a special commemoratin' quilt for the occasion too—white stars on a blue background with red an' white train track stripes across it—though ol' Gray Mary favored a more traditional design.

Of course, Tumblewheeze thought they'd better hurry up an' get the Main Street widened before then—at least to make more room for the parade. Curly an' Q started sellin' train whistle candies at Confectionery World—an' you could hear 'em hootin' all over town. Tasted better'n they sounded though. But they did help drown out Miss Bovine's singin'. I tell you, she practiced bellerin' well into the night. An' then there was them firecrackers. My, oh my!

But it was a different sound altogether that stirred up the town folks about dawn on that Independence Day mornin'.

Cooo-Ka-Rooo.

Cock-La-Diddle-Doo.

Ker-Ricka-Ricka-Roo.

"What's all that racket, J.D.?" asked Rosie, with curlers still in her mane.

"Hmmm," says J.D., "them sounds like roosters to me."

"Must be a whole flock of 'em then," Rosie reckoned.

"I better get down to Bo's house," says J.D., puttin' on his vest, "See you later, Rose." So off he galloped.

When he got to the middle of town, the crowin' was near deafinin'.

Cock-A-Doodle-Dooo!

Karee-Karee-Karooo!

J.D. pounded on Bo's door, "How many roosters you got in there, Bo?"

Bo opened the door, a-hangin' his head. "I count a full dozen, J.D.—an' I've had more'n enough time to check my math."

"I reckon you have, Bo. I reckon you have."

"Can you help me git 'em out of here 'fore I go deaf?"

"I reckon, Bo," answered J.D. "Let's gather 'em up an' take 'em back to Jack's place."

"O.K.," whimpered Bo. "Guess I won't be gettin' them hunerd an' forty-four thousand eggs after all."

"Sorry, Bo, but you know what they says 'bout countin' chickens."

Well, by the time J.D. an' Bo had got them feisty roosters all gathered up an' settled back at Jack's place, the Independence Day festivities was well under way. The *narrow* streets (at least as Tumblewheeze called em') was filled with cactus blossoms an' leftover firecrackers.

"Guess we missed them floats," sighed Bo.

But a band was comin' down the street now, led by none other than Miss Bovine. The townfolks along the boardwalks was a-wavin' flags an' banners—cheerin' 'em on, all the while blowin' on them candied train-whistles for all they was worth. (I guess Curly an' Q was makin' a perty penny that day.)

Then above all that commotion come that long-awaited sound.

Woooo-wooo.

Tumblewheeze ran over an' rang the town bell to git ever'body's attention.

"HOLD EVER'THING!" he shouted. "QUIET! Listen."

Well the band petered out, an' the crowd got quiet—real quiet—quiet as a chicken in an' egg that ain't been hatched yet.

Then it come again.

Woooooo, Woooooo.

"TRAIN'S A-COMIN'!" shouted Tumblewheeze—an' it was like the egg hatched an' the chickens got to squawkin'—with a dozen or more roosters to boot! My what a commotion! The whole town pert' near stumbled all over itself—rushin' out to the train tracks. I think Miss Bovine even trampled the tuba along the way.

WOOOO, WOOOOO.

Well the folks had draped a fancy red ribbon across the tracks for a cuttin' ceremony later, an' ever'body crowded 'round the spot to see the train come to a stop for the first time there in Dust River Gulch. Folks started up their flag an' banner wavin'. They was tootin' them candy-whistles! They was cheerin'. They was all huggin' each other.

WOOOOO, WOOOOO.

The folks on the train leaned out the winders—a-wavin' back an' smilin'. Folks dressed up in fancy duds greetin' all our townfolk. What a picture it was! I ain't never seen Dust River Gulch in a finer state of affairs than it were right at that there moment in time.

"Yahoooo!"

"Welcome, neighbors!"

"Yeehah!"

Firecrackers was goin' off like a twenty-one hunerd gun salute.

WOOOOO, WOOOOOO, Chugga, Chugga, Chug, Chugga, Chugga, Chug.

The train chugged right through that red ribbon stoppin' place.

Wooooo, Wooooo.

The folks on the train kept wavin' an' smilin' as the engine an' the passenger cars passed by. Then come the caboose, with a blue-suited conductor on the back railin', just a-wavin' an' smilin' too.

Only Tumblewheeze, runnin' behind, dared call out the question that had to be on ever'body's mind, "WHERE YA GOIN'?"

"KLONDIKE KANYON," called back the friendly conductor. "THAT'S NEXT STOP ON THE LINE."

Wooooooo, wooooooo . . .

An' just like that, it was all gone. That was more'n a year ago now. Well, I reckon I better get back to my packin'.

Some feller said he'd help move my belongin's over to Klondike Kanyon along with me. It's gettin' to be a perty big town nowadays—Klondike Kanyon. Lots of folks done headed that way lately. An' you know, after a while, it'll prob'ly seem like home too.

The Action Never Dries Up In Dust River Gulch!

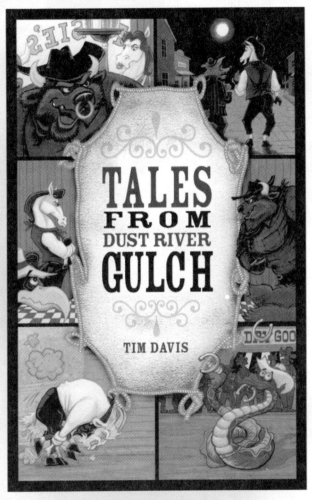

Where the action begins